The Dragon
Lady

Angelique S. Anderson

for putting up with our craggers taste it

The Dragon Lady

Published by Created Angel Design and Publication

Book design copyright © 2017 Angelique S. Anderson

Cover design: Joaquin Nunez

Edited by: William H. Gould

Illustrations: Angel Esqueda, Shevonne Daley

© 2017 Angelique S. Anderson all rights reserved.

ISBN-13: 978-1541395190
ISBN-10: 1541395190

DEDICATION

This book is dedicated to those who
never lost their imagination. To the tinkerers, inventors, crafters and artists.
May your creativity accompany you, no matter what you do. May your
creative mind have the freedom it desires to live, do and be.

Never grow up completely. Life is too beautiful for that.

CONTENTS

ACKNOWLEDGMENTS

First and foremost, to my beautiful family and loving, supportive husband, thank you for all you sacrifice so that I can have a career I love. You are my hero forever. To my children, I simply adore being your mother, thank you for being who you are. Your imagination and creativity is a beautiful thing, please never lose that.

To my 'write or die,' Rose C., my fellow author friend, confidant, rock and shoulder to cry on, you are just everything. Inspiration, friendship, love, strength, laughs… thank you for being who you are and never giving up on me.

To my beautiful friends who have seen me through, Shevonne D., my twin, there are no words! To my bestest Melissa V. you gave me strength when I couldn't. Thank you! I love you ladies dearly, and my life is forever enriched because you are in it.

To my editor, William G., this could never have happened without you. It was my story, but your hand made it something I know we both can believe in. Thank you for your friendship, guidance and the many laughs. You are one of a kind.

To my cover designer, Joaquin N., a tremendous talent, who saw my vision even when I didn't have the words. You brought to life what I could have only hoped for, and I will be forever thankful.

To everyone else, Nikki W., Middagh G., Carrie S., Nancy M., thank you for your support and encouragement! There are so many others I know I am leaving someone out, but trust me that your love and support is felt and appreciated!

Most importantly, to my creator who gives me the talents I have and the courage to use them. I love you and thank you for everything in my life.

CHAPTER ONE

The dim glow from a lone gaslight revealed one flea-bitten rat scampering down the main street of Dobbinsturn Parish, his bewhiskered nose sniffing for crumbs. The rodent's ears perked forward at a strange new sound, then he raised his head to sniff an interesting aroma wafting to him on the breeze.

Given any common sense at all, the furry little beast would have kept running, but it was his fate that landed him in the knife-sharp claws of the most glorious white dragon a rat may ever hope to see. If rats hoped for such things, that is.

The radiant white dragon spent the night soaring over the boroughs of London, his iridescent scales glowing under the gentlest cast of moonlight. The putrid stench of black death invaded his nostrils as he swooped down and grabbed the wriggling rat in his claws, tossing it into his mouth without chewing and swallowing the gamey little thing whole.

One final act of goodwill. The white dragon wasn't sure of his end, but he felt it closing in on his sickly body. He doubted he would even have the strength to fly after this eve.

As if on cue, the surrounding atmosphere changed, he felt the presence of his dark counterpart like a fog that descended upon his beloved London. He sucked in a deep breath through his large scaly nostrils, wishing to savor this moment for all of eternity. There was no doubt he would miss the sights and smells of Earth.

His black enemy swooped down upon him, its massive horns and prismatic scales invisible to human eyes against the backdrop of night.

The black dragon pulled up short of him, its glistening scales in stark contrast with his white ones, giving a small hint at just how opposite they were. As if he was able to hear the gods speak of the end himself, his heart palpitated nervously. Once, long ago, he would have been strong enough to fight this foe, but that time had long since passed. Age and illness robbed him of the strength he once possessed.

As if in a dream, he watched the enemy dragon as it swooped to the street, attacking a staggering drunk whose only mistake was showing himself in the lamplight. He wanted to fight it. It was his job to do so, but he knew the beast would kill him before he was able to stop him, so he watched helplessly as the black monster gathered a mouthful of the man, its massive jaws closing over his body and mashing the drunk's upper torso to juicy bits.

"Don't do this!" The pearl white dragon called out, a tear squeezing from one wrinkled eye as he watched the blood of the man drip over the chin of his evil opposite. His dark counterpart only chuckled to himself before he dropped what was left of the stranger's body to the ground, making a squelching sound as it hit the cobblestones. The sight of it would make anyone squeamish, including the pure-hearted dragon, unable to stop the senseless slaughter.

The angry black beast flew towards him, eyes flashing crimson with hatred.

"Why must you take an innocent life?" The white dragon tried to reason, but his enemy merely opened his jaws wide, spewing a blast of fire in his direction. Too sick and too old to dodge the flames, he didn't even try to avoid the inevitable impact but instead allowed the fire to engulf him from horn to tail. His glorious body plummeted to the ground, hitting the road with crushing force, extinguishing most of the flames with the impact.

As the victor his enemy chuckled to himself and flew out of sight, a small pocket watch device hanging on a chain around the white dragon's neck flipped open. A tiny, magical, bronze dragon with cloaking ability crawled out and dusted himself off. He scanned the area, worried that wakeful eyes may have heard the one-sided battle and been drawn to investigate. Seeing that the large white dragon was on fire, he blew a gust of wind from his tiny lips strong enough to create a small hurricane.

Once the fire was extinguished, the little bronze beast set about trying to heal his injured friend, but it was too late. The heartbeat grew weaker until it ceased altogether. As his friend breathed his last, a soft glow of blue essence rose from the body, like a tiny dancing flame, and shot through the night toward its human host. Meanwhile, the lifeless dragon body had disappeared altogether.

The tiny bronze dragon grew larger and flew after the blue light until it entered a small dwelling in a rundown neighborhood. The tiny dancing flame came to rest on an aging man, who lay still as stone on a bed. When the flame entered the man's body, his chest heaved with a deep breath, but it was his final one. The tiny dragon sat on the edge of the bed, his scaly clawed hand resting on the wrinkled human one. His deep emerald eyes were wet with tears.

Goodbye, dear friend, you have served the gods well.

He then returned to his place inside the pocket watch device and willed the device to be magically transported back to its hiding place until it was time to be revealed once more.

"Father, are you alright?" Wylie Petford had grown used to hearing her father call for her in the early morning, the absence of his voice sent her heart reeling. No, no! Please, not yet!

Wylie rushed to his room, fear taking precedence over rational thought. The past few weeks were hard on him as he clung tenuously to life. Heaven only knew how long the herbal treatments would continue working if they were working at all. She felt his forehead, which was damp with sweat and used a rag to dab it dry.

Nicholas Petford did not stir beneath her touch, and she assumed for the moment that he was sleeping peacefully until she realized there was something unnatural about his stillness.

"Father… Father are you well?" Panic setting in, she began fervently pressing his chest. The rise and fall that should be occurring naturally as he breathed in and out was absent.

"Father, please, wake up!" She slapped his face lightly, several times in rapid succession, willing that he would wake and get cross with her for doing such a thing. When there was no response, and even his cheek felt cold to her touch, she realized that her worst fears had been realized.

She gently stroked his whiskered cheek, her heart screaming silently at his cold, still form. Any minute now he would awaken, and ask for fresh biscuits and jam as he did every morning, but she knew there was no use fighting it.

He had been sick for such a long time, and Dr. Antony Flack's medicine was more effective than promised. It had kept her father alive for much longer than most patients. She would have to thank him personally for the miracle provided through his tinctures.

A million thoughts assaulted Wylie's mind as she cried. There was no doubt about the difficulty of the past few months. The continuous need for medications for her father and loss of wages had taken their toll. Though it was no doubt better than the alternative which was now a reality. She would have to find the strength to ask her employer to take time away from work to lay her father to rest.

Her employer, very gracious until now, would surely understand that even the poor grieve their dead.

She did not expect kindness, but she indeed hoped for it. She lay on the cold stone floor, her face buried in her arms as the tears fell until she finally drifted off to sleep.

As one life left Earth and ascended into heaven, another being was rising into the night sky in glorious form. Its wingspan as long as three men laid from head to toe. It opened its magnificent jaws, and an inferno of fire and sulfurous smells blazed forth like a volcano giving birth. Though it was the dead of night, the dark shadow that now took to the skies was not unseen by the local pet population. Afar off, the lowing of cattle could be heard as they milled about frantically, afraid for their lives.

Hours before…

Near the border of upper Dobbinsturn and Kinnemore, a newly purchased and renovated tavern was alive with raucous laughter and cheers from its new inhabitants and patrons. In a rather unusual move, the tavern had been named after its financier, Lord Jameston Ukridge, rather than its owner. Ukridge Tavern was an establishment that the owner, Dorian Gilligan, hoped would be passed down for generations.

The elaborate interior boasted of its owner's airship travels, with strong stone beams and rustic archways reminiscent of the stone chapels in France and Germany. A former first mate and a man with excellent taste, Dorian made sure the Ukridge tavern represented the life he once lived.

Between the elegant stone archways, the walls held a vast array of art and design; glorious pieces collected during Dorian's airship travels around the world with his friend and captain, Daggert Kingsley. The floor had been expertly laid with the richest of mahogany wood, and the glasses that slid across the freshly polished wood counter were full to the brim of the best homemade ale the patrons from Dobbinsturn and Kinnemore had ever tasted.

As proud as Dorian Gilligan was of his new business venture, he was even more proud of his friend Captain Daggert. For it was that very night that Captain Daggert traded in his captain's hat for a more dapper one. He'd recently sold his fabulous airship to the highest bidder, and in celebration, he'd bought a round of drinks for all those in attendance at the tavern that eve.

"Twenty years have I been a Captain. Seventeen of those years I've been honored and privileged to sail with one of the best first mates who ever crewed an airship, my first mate Dorian Gilligan."

He raised his mug to toast him. "You're a fine man and a hell of a partner, and I wish you the best on your new venture. Now, it's high time I invested in a new undertaking. That is why I am taking my purse and heading to the Strand. Perhaps I will attend the Queen's court, or I will live in the streets… a penniless artist, begging for alms! Either way, the winds have changed for me." He raised his glass to the crowd of patrons. "Drinks for one and all, on me!"

"Here! Here!" The sounds of clinking glass followed the salute as he tossed a clinking coin purse on the counter for payment. The echoes of the men's 'hurrahs' followed the former captain as he wobbled out onto the street full as a tick and pockets flush with a coin.

A flask of celebration still in hand, he ambled carelessly down the cobblestones, hardly able to make out the stones of the road ahead of him until he collided head-on with a sturdy metal lamp post, its dim light barely casting a shadow about him.

"Excuse me, m'Lady." He laughed, patting the post tenderly and tipping his hat before continuing to walk along the cobbled avenue. Overhead the flapping of great wings caught his ear. Though he was not in his clearest mindset and his eyes not fully adjusted to the darkness, he did raise his head to look upward, barely making out the shape of something so black that its form temporarily blocked the light of the moon. So, it was that the moment he saw the black form, it was too late.

The new wind that carried him was a cruel one indeed. For no sooner had he traded in his Captain's hat than he now joined the ranks of the deceased. His murderer leaving the lower half of his body on the cobblestones only to be discovered the next morning by the one person who would be able to identify the coin purse and boots that were left behind; his former first mate Dorian Gilligan.

CHAPTER TWO

The great airship parade had all of lower London mafficking about like a herd of wild horses. Wylie stepped back from the window and stood next to the bed that had been her father's. She straightened the bedclothes for the millionth time and wished that she was able to take his aging hand in hers just once more.

It killed her to know that his body was buried with others of her same station in life. It was quite possible grave-robbers had already dug it up and stolen his shoes and maybe even his clothing. It made her feel good though, to know that the little money she'd been able to save had been enough to buy him a decent coffin.

She'd even been able to afford a real priest, and even though only a few people from the tiny Anglican Parish of Lugwallow attended, she was content, knowing she wasn't alone in the cemetery as they lowered him into the ground. She'd done right by him, and that was all she could have hoped for.

"I do wish you were able to see what I see, father," Wylie spoke out loud, wishing he could hear her. "The cavalcade of airships is simply brilliant this year." Her eyes teared up unexpectedly, and she wiped the droplets away. She knew it was brought on by the realization that they would never again share the joy and awe of watching the annual Airshow together. The Airshow was truly one of the best things about living in their poor little town. They had the finest view of it without having to deal with a cluster of Londonites tallying about.

"All right father, I'm off to tend to Lord Adrian's horses, I shall return before nightfall," she said to the empty bed. How many times had he chided her for lollygaggin' about Dobbinsturn when she was late returning from the stable?

She'd always countered, "But how else am I to find a worthy suitor?" to which he'd jokingly replied a time or two, "Perhaps if you didn't smell like a stable, a suitor would come to you." Her reply was always the same, "If he's a worthy suitor, he will not mind such things." Then she would giggle and kiss him gently on his wrinkled forehead.

"That's the kind of talk that will scare them all away," he would whisper weakly, always smiling, always teasing. He continued teasing right up until the day he died. She sighed heavily, leaving his room and closing the door behind her.

"I miss you, father."

She grabbed her Wellingtons, sliding the worn rubber over her straight-legged trousers. To an outsider, the boots were past their prime, but to Wylie, they were protection from the manure and straw that poked her legs. There was another reason she couldn't part with them though; she would never admit out loud that the old boots were her prized possession which once belonged to Lord Adrian.

Wylie shrugged off the sudden thought of him, and pinned up her wild, untamed ginger hair in a loose braid, then slid her hand-fashioned goggles over the top of her head, adjusting the mini-periscope that had come loose from its clip. A carefree glance in the aged antique mirror in the entryway told her that her goggles were slightly off kilter. She straightened them, sucking in a deep breath.

I must find the strength to get through today.

She traced her fingers over the goggles, pausing on the worn leather sides. They needed new straps and to be re-sewn. Too much time had gone by since she'd shown them the attention they deserved.

There was a soft spot in Wylie's heart for her goggles. She'd hand sewn them using bits of leather from an old pair of her father's boots whose soles had finally come undone. Then scrounging about and using her meager earnings, she purchased the lenses, three on the right for different levels of magnification, and two on the left specially made for seeking out the constellations. Dark brass adorned the eye frames and the periscope clip as she had a long-standing affinity for dark brass.

She would cherish them even more now as her father had been so proud that she created them on her own. It was perhaps the last thing he'd praised her for, and his approval always meant the world to her. She grabbed her hip pouch, pulling it over her petite frame so it rested snugly on her side as she stepped out into the brisk morning air.

The door banged shut behind her driven by the cool wind swirling about, the crumbling old door with the aging brass knob barely catching on the lock. Her home was in desperate need of repair, but it had been all she could do to keep food on the table and a roof over their heads lately.

Her father's medicine took most of her meager stable girl earnings month after month. She never complained though since it was much better to have him still alive and breathing for the time left to him. Perhaps now that her father had passed on, it would do her some good to fix up their home. It was hard for her to imagine ever giving it up. As long as she was there, she could visit his bedroom and breathe deep of his fading presence. It didn't even bother her that she may die a spinster with no real hope of love or family.

"Come now, Wyles. No need to think upon such things," she told herself out loud as she focused on the hours walk ahead of her into the grand Parish of Dobbinsturn, to Lord Adrian's estate.

Perhaps if Adrian were not a Lord, or she not just a mere stable hand, he would make a lovely suitor. She was quite content to replace sad thoughts of her father's absence and negative thoughts of being alone with images of Lord Adrian's lovely, chiseled face and lively eyes.

His eyes were her favorite feature by far. His bewitching gray-eyed gaze tripped her up more than once, causing a soft pink to caress her cheeks before she realized she'd paused in her work just to stare at him. She refused to let herself forget though that she would never be fit for a man such as him. Of course, it was true that the gentle-natured Lord Adrian was already betrothed to Lady

Judith, her persnickety, but gloriously wonderful, nearest and dearest friend.

How Wylie both adored and felt jealous of Lady Judith Ukridge. The two of them had been friends for ages, to Lord Jameston's dismay. Judith's father made no attempt to hide his distaste for the peasant girl whenever she came to call. Even though he was one of the most well-respected men in all of Dobbinsturn Parish, and even most of London, Wylie found him to be a bit of a mean ol' reprobate and she never hid her opinion of him either. The sudden turning of her thoughts to that contemptible man reminded Wylie that perhaps she should call upon Lady Judith before she headed to the stables.

Judith tried her best to comfort her when Nicolas Petford passed away, but Judith's father forbade her to attend the funeral. He insisted that his daughter never be seen in such a place as the lowly Parish of Lugwallow. This only heightened Wylie's dislike for the awful man all the more, but regardless, the young ladies managed to keep a close friendship.

Judith's home was a bit out of her way, a fact which Wylie relished as her time spent in Dobbinsturn was always too short. Any excuse to stay longer on its cobblestone streets filled her with happiness. As she approached the familiar cream-colored mansion, it took her breath away as always. The grandness of it never ceased to amaze her, with its octagon pillars and over-sized windows looking out onto the bustling streets of one of the loveliest parts of all London.

Wylie took a deep breath and ascended the elegant marble steps that Lord Jameston Ukridge had specially commissioned. He was a boastful man, and from the day she first met him, he often spoke of his wealth. After all, he was one of the most sought after airship architects in London. He was responsible for designing nearly half of the queen's air fleet, a fact he seldom let anyone forget.

After Judith's mother had passed from consumption, her father set aside his career to take care of Judith. Muddling about at home, he'd developed an interest in houses for sale, which in turn resulted in his selling houses as a business. He even, as he'd earnestly stated to her, would go so far as to help new business owners acquire land and loaned them money to build on the property. It wasn't long before he purchased a building of his own to open a bank. He called it Ukridge Business and Loan and became even richer because of it. Another fact which he never let Wylie forget.

Reaching the first step, she knocked gently on the door and waited patiently for someone to answer. Shortly the curtain parted at a window to her left, and there was her best friend peeking out, waving and smiling at her.

"Darling Judith. God love her." Wylie waved and smiled back, adjusting her leather vest over her waistline and her utility belt, with its multiple pockets and gadget holders, resting snugly against her hips. The door swung open, and Hildreth Mackinson gave her a most unwelcome glare. She turned her back on the guest without even so much as a second glance at Wylie, which made her laugh.

"Oh come now, Hildreth. Still don't fancy me, darling?" The sound of feet hurriedly stamping away was the only response.

"Oh, my dearest Wylie. Have you come to send my house into a tizzy?" Judith teased, but in her eyes, the gleam of something calamitous flashed.

"You know that is my greatest joy," Wylie teased back, hugging her friend. Her stomach flipped unsettlingly. Something about Judith's voice warned her to be worried, but she was unable to fathom the reason. When they stepped away from each other, they both remained smiling, but there was a tension so thick it could be cut with a shiv. "I see your housekeeper has not let her fondness for me get in the way of her household duties," she winked at Judith, slipping her thumbs behind her belt for comfort.

"I'm afraid that is the least of your worries, dear friend."

A million scenarios ran through Wylie's mind, though they all seemed a bit unmitigated. She was letting her imagination get away with her.

"What Judith? What it is it?"

"Not here. Not now. I know you have only just put your father in the ground, but terrible things are afoot. You must go! I will find you!" With that, the one person in all the world who made Wylie feel like she wasn't alone, was pushing her out the door. When she tried to protest, Judith's eyes welled up with tears. "I promise, I will explain! Go!" Without ceremony Judith shoved Wylie roughly out the door and slammed it, leaving Wylie shocked and bewildered by her friend's behavior.

CHAPTER THREE

London looked just as it had a moment ago; crowds of people milling about, and the sky parade still in full swing. Nothing had changed, and yet everything had changed. Wylie couldn't remember a single moment in all the years she'd known Lady Judith when her friend had acted in such a way. A typical person perhaps would not think anything of it, but Wylie felt as if she couldn't breathe. She turned to glance back up the steps, seeking out the window in the hope that she was being beckoned back inside, but the curtains were drawn and still. The house was as silent as a tomb from where she stood.

Oh Judith, what is it? What has happened? Her eyes began to well with tears. She could handle being alone, but not her best friend being angry or upset with her.

Stop over thinking it, Wylie, she tried to convince herself. The reminder that she still had a job to go to interrupted her thoughts. *Yes, work. I must trust that Judith will find me and tell me what this is all about.* She convinced herself to let that be enough, and with time slipping away, she hurriedly made her way to Lord Adrian's stables. She knew that the days she had taken off to bury her father would drastically affect her workload, and the last thing she wanted was to anger her employer.

As Wylie rushed to Lord Adrian's home, the sight of the tall wrought iron fences was a welcome sight for her troubled heart. Slipping through the gate as stealthily as possible, she rushed straight to the stables. The smell of horse manure had reached her nose before she was inside, but even that was comforting to her. This was something she was able to fix. Something she had some control over, and the time she spent shoveling was a welcome break from the thoughts of her father dying and her friend's mysterious behavior.

After dunging out the stalls and spreading fresh straw so that the horses had a comfortable place to lay down as the weather got colder, she grabbed a halter to put on the stallion, Chaos. By far the wildest and the least broke of the bunch, he was still her favorite. His jet-black coat always glowed after she brushed him, and for as long as Wylie had worked there as a stablehand, he had never given her a bit of trouble.

There was something in his spirit that she connected with, and she always gave him extra attention. She often brought him an apple or fresh carrots when her meager earnings would allow. She gently pulled the halter over his head and fastened the buckles securely. He nickered softly as she did so, nudging his head against her.

"Affection? Why Chaos, I've never seen this side of you," she joked, gently stroking his mane as he stomped his hooves in response. Standing on her tiptoes, she wrapped her arms around his muscled neck as if he were a dear friend she hadn't seen in ages. Then she let out all of her frustration and sadness in great wracking sobs that scared the mares as they all started whinnying and nickering in their stalls. Chaos didn't move, and instead, laid his head on her shoulder while she cried.

When she had finished crying, she wiped her eyes, grabbed the brushes, and began grooming him.

"Ahem," Lord Adrian cleared his throat behind her. At the sound, Wylie's face turned several shades of red, and she inhaled sharply.

"You couldn't have told me he was here?" she whispered to Chaos.

"Do not worry yourself, Wylie. Your secret is safe with me."

"What secret?" Her cheeks went red with embarrassment. She hadn't meant to get emotional, and she surely didn't want Lord Adrian thinking that of her. She continued brushing the stallion's shiny coat.

"Exactly. However, I guess that answers my question." He crossed the stable floor, kicking straw out of his way as he approached her.

"What question is that, Lord Adrian?"

Coming up behind her, he laid a gloved hand on her shoulder and turned her to face him. Her breath caught in her throat as even through leather she felt the warmth of his hand there. She dared not speak or breathe or even move for fear he would remove it.

"I desperately wanted to ask how you were doing… it turns out Chaos knows you better than I do, which, I have to say, makes me a bit jealous," he smiled sincerely at her. She couldn't bring herself to say a word. Has the whole world gone mad? When she didn't respond, he said, "That bad, huh? Can't say I blame you, Wyles. I don't know how you're managing. If my father passed... I would simply…" She saw by the emotion on his face that he couldn't bring himself to even think about it.

"Well, no worries about that, my Lord. Your father is as healthy as a horse," she joked, hoping to break the unwelcome sadness that had entered the conversation. Lord Adrian, his hand still resting awkwardly on her shoulder, used his free hand to grab one of hers.

"Wylie, I don't want you to feel that you're alone because you're not. I still consider you a friend, and if there is ever anything I can do for you, don't hesitate to ask." Their eyes locked, and he stepped in closer. For a brief moment, it felt like he might lean in to kiss her, though she hadn't the faintest idea why. Not that I would stop him. He brushed the hair back from her forehead, and the moment felt magical. All the feelings she had been holding back because of his betrothal to her best friend, broke out of the carefully guarded recesses of her mind.

Dang blammit, Wylie. You warned yourself not to fall for him. You've been doing so well… why now? But there was no answer. She had spent many months worried about her father, barely able to pay for his medicine and put food on the table. All bets are off, just don't do anything imprudent, she warned herself. Not that she would do anything irresponsible, she would never do anything to hurt her best friend, but there was nothing wrong with allowing herself to feel something, was there? Especially if it meant that for a brief moment out of each day, she could be happy. It was perhaps the only happiness she had left.

Just as that thought crossed from her mind, Wylie caught movement out of the corner of one eye. She whirled to see Lady Judith, arms folded across her chest, standing in the stable entrance. In a panic, she stepped away from Lord Adrian, who bowed to her and then hurried to Lady Judith's side.

"My betrothed!" he exclaimed, his mouth turning up in a most glorious smile. To Wylie's delight and dismay, Lord Adrian took Lady Judith's hand in his and raised it to his lips. "How is that I should be so lucky as to see both my good friend and my wife-to-be on the same day?" Wylie being referred to as 'friend' drew a look from Judith, but it made Wylie positively giddy. "What is it that brings you here today?"

Judith didn't seem in a hurry to answer that question and instead shot daggers toward Wylie.

"My beloved," she spoke to Lord Adrian. "I have private business with Miss Petford. Would you be a dear, and excuse us, just for a moment?"

"Absolutely." He leaned in and kissed Judith's cheek, though the gesture seemed to be more one of obligation than love or adoration. When he had left the two women alone, Judith was first to break the silence.

"Mind telling me what the hell that was all about, Wylie?"

"My dear Judith, you know full well I have never kept a thing from you and I would never hurt you. You've known from the beginning that I adore Lord Adrian." Judith gasped in shock. "As a friend," Wylie added fervently. "Though he is lovely to look at. Please, I beg of you... give pause to what you think happened. He is a Lord... and I am a foul-smelling stable girl. For goodness' sake, I clean up his horse's droppings. Surely you don't think he would be interested in me in the slightest?" Reason gave Judith the clarity she needed, Wylie saw it on her face.

"Nonetheless, you two were very close. Surely, you must not be that foul-smelling if he was able to stand being so near to you."

"My father did just pass away, and perhaps as he said, he does indeed see me as a friend for he was simply asking me in the sincerest of tones how I was dealing with my father's death. I have not lied to you Judith, nor would I ever. Charming and handsome as he may be, my best friend is marrying him, and I couldn't be happier for you."

Lady Judith's cheeks glowed crimson. "Dear Wylie, I am so sorry. I don't know what I was thinking. Come here..." she gathered her in a hug and held her tight. "I've been so ludicrously selfish. Your father just died... I don't know what's the matter with me?" The smell of flowers wafted to Wylie's nose, and she welcomed it. She had been craving a hug from her best friend for several days; so much so that a lump rose in that back of her throat and tears threatened to spring up again, but she held them back.

"I've missed you, Judith. The ceremony was small but lovely. I wish you had been able to be there. How are you? What is going on? Why did you throw me out of your house so quickly, earlier?"

"Oh dear," Judith ended their hug by pushing Wylie in front of her. "Please don't hate me for what I am about to say."

"What? Goodness' sake, what is it, Judith?"

"It's my father. He's found two investors, and the three of them are planning to purchase Lugwallow Parish."

"What?" Wylie stared at her in dismay, but her friend just looked down at the floor in abject silence.

CHAPTER FOUR

"What?" Wylie asked again.

Still no answer.

"Well, that's good news, isn't it? That means someone with money is going to purchase Lugwallow Parish and clean it up, right? That means that perhaps all the families that live there may receive proper housing, correct?"

"Oh, dearest Wylie, I wish I could tell you that my father had only the best of intentions, but I am afraid it is quite the opposite."

"Stop being so cryptic, just lay it out!"

"Dang blammit it all, Wylie; it's not easy to tell my best friend, that my father wants to acquire her home. He wants to acquire all the homes in Lugwallow so the families can be booted out into the streets and the homes can be knocked down to make way for new businesses and upper-class society!" Breathless, Lady Judith covered her mouth and stepped back.

"Surely you must be jesting, Judith? Please tell me you're jesting? Surely your father wouldn't do that to innocent people?" Her voice rose an octave. "Tell me he would not destroy the lives of children and the old and the sick, all for his own monetary gain?"

"I would like nothing better. I wish it were all in fun, but it's not. You must warn the families! You must get them somewhere safe!"

Wylie couldn't bring herself to speak for the moment, the thought rolled through her mind of old Thomas Wilfred Fleming, the Vicar she paid her rent to. She knew that he was getting up in age, but she had always assumed he would pass the church and the parish of Lugwallow down to his son. Why hadn't he told her he was selling Lugwallow off?

"Judith, some of those miserable little homes are all those people have in the world. I am not about to tell them to leave, but I can guarantee if your father tries to take our homes, he is going to have a fight on his hands. I may be only one person, but so help me… I will fight to the death for those people! How dare he take advantage of a good man like the Vicar?"

"You stubborn arse!" Judith shouted at her. "You're going to lose everything; don't you get it? Everything! Please get out of there while you still can! You have no idea the influence my father has. He could send you to jail!"

"Then let him send me because he's not getting mine or anyone else's dwelling without losing some of his favorite body parts."

Judith gasped, tears welling up in her face. "I was trying to help you!"

"Sounds like you were trying to help your father more, eh? Clear out the houses… make it easier for him to move in. I don't think so. We're done here." For the first time in their entire friendship. Wylie realized why Lord Jameston had discouraged their camaraderie. Lady Judith and Wylie came from two different worlds.

Two worlds that would most likely never merge peacefully without a full-blown war between the classes, much like the one Wylie imagined was going to happen if Ukridge tried to take their homes.

She didn't know how or when, but she was going to stop him. She may still be a bit young, but she was no chavy of a girl anymore. She was a woman and she would fight for what was hers, even if it meant giving up all of her wages to the vicar so that he would not sell off Lugwallow.

Wylie finished brushing the mares' coats, all four of them, after tucking Chaos back in his stall with fresh bedding and a manger full of hay. Then she filled their feed bins for the night and kissed their noses before heading home. All the while she was thinking of how she would present the issue to the people of Lugwallow. She only hoped they were willing to fight for what was rightfully theirs.

Whether it was sleep deprivation or the loss of her father still weighing heavily on her heart as Wylie walked home, feelings of dread came unbidden. She wasn't normally one to be anxious, but she highly distrusted Lord Jameston, and her mind began to fill with all sorts of possible violent scenarios.

Only moments before she had felt certain she would be willing to fight Lord Ukridge tooth and nail. Now fear gradually became an overwhelming force.

Of course, the Vicar would refuse my wages? Obviously, it's nowhere near what he would get from Lord Jameston. What if I do rally the people of Lugwallow against him? He'll likely have us all jailed? What about the children who are too young to care for themselves? What about the widow Turpin? As stubborn as that woman is she won't last a day in a moldy cell on rations of dry bread and dirty water.

That's if Lord Jameston is feeling generous. He might just as well have us all hanged, including Thomas Fleming. Maybe I shouldn't fight him? Maybe I should just run? But then he wins. Papa, I wish you were here. I don't know what to do. If you were here, you would tell me what to do to make this right.

Wylie covered the distance in short order as her pace quickened and her thoughts raced. Leave her beloved home? It was almost too much to comprehend. It was all she had left of her father, and yet his death made her home just a sad memory. Maybe it would be better for all of them to pick up and move while they had the chance to do so.

Maybe moving will give us the fresh start we so desperately need. So much loss, so much death. The consumption has taken so many of us. Perhaps a new place to live will give us hope. We haven't had hope in a long time. Yet, I can't see myself leaving Lugwallow. My beloved Lugwallow. If only Lord Jameston would help us fix up our homes and stay in them. Wylie already knew that Lugwallow Parish was an eyesore, but she dearly loved the Parson Thomas Fleming and knew that it was his age, not his lack of desire to fix things, that kept it in disrepair. If only she could plead her case to a higher-up, but that would be wasted efforts.

Wylie arrived home so quickly, she was hardly able to remember the journey. Her thoughts burned with the possibilities of what it would take for her people to fight against a man such as Lord Jameston and win. She knew that the people of Lugwallow would not just follow her blindly into battle against him. His name was too well known as was his lack of compassion.

Part of her wanted to riot against Lord Ukridge, to cause a revolt in Lugwallow. A demonstration so boisterous that the surrounding boroughs would have to sit up and take notice. Another part of her wanted to petition someone greater than she to side with them, someone who would see their plight and take up their cause. Then there was the small nagging voice in the back of her head, the one that in some respects believed what Lady Judith had said about Lord Jameston having Wylie sent to prison, or worse.

She finally came to the conclusion that in order to keep her people safe, she would have to leave. I cannot stay here. I must leave before he comes and takes what little I have left. The people of Lugwallow will have to fight of their accord, or get out, just as I am doing.

In haste, she began to clean out her father's room.

Better to save a few of my father's memories than to lose them all to the likes of Lord Jameston.

Hot tears threatened her eyes. What is happening to me? Where was the strong, self-assured woman who had cared for a sick and dying man for months? The one who had worked so hard to keep a roof over their heads in spite of the fact that she was a woman. She had fed them and even found time to sew and work on gadgets that would better aid her in accomplishing her job in a more efficient manner. At the drop of a hat, she was just going to pack her things and leave? She pulled her father's meager belongings of two shirts and two pairs of trousers from his single chest of drawers.

The smell of him clung to his clothes as if he were still standing right there.

If only he were.

She desperately needed him; needed his help. Leaving Lugwallow to start a new life somewhere else, alone, was not something a woman typically did. Unless they were women of the world, or 'fallen women,' something Wylie would never even consider. Not even if she were completely penniless. She would lay dying on the cobbled streets, begging for crumbs before she would find herself in one of those seedy bordellos, like the ones the men in Dobbinsturn liked to frequent.

Wylie laid out a sheet on her father's bed, placing his shirts on it. She would have to leave the beloved dresser behind or pass it on to one of her neighbors. As she pushed each drawer back into place, in the dresser that her father himself had built when she was just a girl, she heard a solid clunk within the last drawer.

Wylie slammed the drawer shut again and once more heard the clunk against the oak. She pulled the drawer out and ran her hand around the inside. The weak light of the oil lamp barely illuminated the space, but she was able to detect nothing but smooth wood beneath her fingertips.

Dragging the drawer all the way out she flipped it over, and noticed on the lower left side, near the back, was a small perfect square of dark wood... She knew by its flawless shape that it was not just a chance knot in the wood. Someone had done it on purpose. As she passed her fingers over it, she could feel the tiniest hint of an edge. She used her fingernail to pry at it and as she did so the dark colored square slid open to reveal a small compartment. Then, something solid dropped to the floor.

She picked it up, feeling the weight and shape of it, and determined that it was a pocket watch of some sort. She made her way to her father's bed and sat down close to the oil lamp. By the light of the lamp, she discovered it was indeed a pocket watch case, heavily detailed with a gorgeous aged bronze exterior. A dragon emblem took up the entirety of the front, and its wings opened to reveal the watch face.

Only, as it turned out, it wasn't a watch. The dragon wings made up the front of the case, and the head that stretched over the top gripped a chain in its fanged mouth. As the wings came open, the watch face was revealed, except where there should be numbers, there were signs and symbols of stars and moons. The moons were in their different stages, and in the center of it was the metallic cut-out of a flying dragon.

On the top of the case was a small brass knob which looked very much like a winding stem, only when she tried to wind it, the wings of the dragon spread wide and a mechanical arm moved a small shiny cog wheel into position over the face of the device. The cog wheel had tiny holes along its rim that lined up with points on the watch face.

"It's like a constellation!" Wylie exclaimed. She knew all about constellations as she adored studying them. However, this was unlike any constellation she had ever seen.

She knew that the device must be of great importance, for her father had kept it hidden from her. To her knowledge, he had never hidden anything from her in her life. Why this? She knew as soon as sunlight hit her pillow in the morning, she would travel into Dobbinsturn to find a clockmaker who might tell her its origin. Until she figured out why her father had gone to extraordinary lengths to keep it hidden, she would keep it secret and tell no one how she'd acquired it. She was sure it had to be worth a considerable sum, and that was something that would be useful against Lord Jameston.

Perhaps this is nothing more than Father's bauble of last resort. He may have intended to use it in an emergency which would explain why he kept it hidden. It will probably fetch a pretty penny, and maybe even help the people of Lugwallow. Maybe this is what would save my small parish! I could give the money to the Vicar! On second thought, would I be able to do that?

For the moment, the emotions of the day caught up with Wylie and managed to distract her from leaving immediately. She lay back on her father's bed, curling up on top of the clothes she'd set apart to take with her, closed her eyes, and drifted off to sleep.

CHAPTER FIVE

Sun, shining through the cracks in the shutters woke Wylie quite abruptly from slumber. Her legs and arms still tired from shoveling manure the day before, she blinked away bits of sleep from her eyes and yawned widely. When she looked for the shirts and things she had laid out she discovered she had knocked them all on the floor in her sleep. As she bent to pick them up, something heavy fell forward around her neck, practically dragging her over the edge of the bed.

"The pocket watch!" She bolted upright in bed and realized that the night before she had curled up and fallen asleep on top of the clothes she'd been sorting. But try as she might, she couldn't remember undressing before dropping off to sleep, nor could she remember changing into her night clothes and climbing into bed. Then again, she tended to forget a great many things lately. Where on Earth were her clothes? When had she taken them off? She yanked off her night clothes, grabbed one of her father's long-sleeved button-up shirts, and pulled it around her before noticing the crumpled heap of clothing on the floor

How did those get there?

At that precise moment, a solid thumping came from the front door.

"Goodness, I suppose it's going to be one of those days." Who on earth could be knocking on her door? She had already sent the doctor away a few days ago when she'd informed him of her father's death. Lady Judith dare not come to the slums of Lugwallow; her delicate sensibilities would not be able to handle getting dirt on her fancy lace dress and expensive leather gallies.

"Just a moment, please. I'm not decent," she yelled out, desperately searching for her clothes. There, her good pants were folded neatly and sitting atop the dresser. She picked up her shirt from the floor, and realized it wouldn't do, as it reeked of yesterday's stable cleaning. She pulled her trousers on and hurriedly buttoned them, leaving her father's shirt unbuttoned and flowing carelessly. She cast a wistful glance toward her trusty corset, knowing she didn't have time to get it on and fastened. So she settled with fastening as many buttons on her father's shirt as possible as she rushed to the door.

The thumping sounded again before she could reach it.

"One moment, I'm on my way," she called out. As she reached for the brass knob and pulled the door inward, she was shocked to find Lord Adrian standing there, his face downcast. Chaos stood behind him tied to a broken street lamp.

"Lord Adrian, why … whatever are you doing here?" She cast a furtive glance up and down the street, worried what people may think. "Please, please … come in ... though I can hardly imagine what a man like you, would want in a place like this?" What will people say? Worse yet, why is he really here? "Please tell me you have not come here to relieve me of my duties as your stable hand?"

Her eyebrows furrowed with worry, and she studied his face to gauge his reaction. He remained where he was, standing silently. Looking down the street, his gaze focused on something in the distance, though she wasn't quite able to make it out.

He looked quite dapper in his black top hat and calf-length frock coat. On closer inspection, she noted that his shirt remained untucked and that he had not bothered to wear a waistcoat. The lack of care he had taken with his wardrobe was a cause of great concern for her. He was always dressed to the nines, even when visiting the stables or riding Chaos.

"Lord Adrian! Whatever has happened? Are you all right?" He shook his head no and stumbled into her house. Realizing that she had more than just his reputation to worry about, she peeked out the door once more, looking for the prying gaze of her neighbors. She was about to duck back inside when she spotted the one person who would judge her most severely.

The widow Nettie Turpin was in front of her home, sweeping the stoop as she did every morning. She didn't even nod in Wylie's direction, Well, let her think what she wants, the old bag, she decided, and hurried back inside, shutting the door before turning to face Lord Adrian.

"My apologies Wylie, I know you've only just lost your father … but I didn't know who else to turn to. I was so lost … I just wanted somewhere to go where I wouldn't be judged." She knew he was fighting hard to keep his composure. It was plain in his face and stormy gray eyes.

"What is it, Lord Adrian … please? Is there anything I can do to help?"

His gaze met hers, and she dared not move for fear of breaking it.

"My father, he's …" he seemed lost for words.

"Has something happened to your father?" She crossed the room to him, wanting desperately to ease whatever was ailing him.

"My father has passed." The words took the breath out of him, and she watched him visibly deflate. She placed her arm into the crook of his and led him to an old faded floral print settee that had been in the home longer than Wylie herself. He collapsed onto it, and silent tears began to trickle down his cheeks.

"Oh, I am so terribly sorry!" To hell with what was right and proper. She sat on the settee next to him, as close as possible without touching him. Taking his hand in hers, she stroked it gently. She was aware of all the rules she was breaking; how her father would scold her for such a thing.

"Forgive me, but what are you doing here? Shouldn't you be mourning with your family, and ..." She didn't even want to say the words out loud but knew she must. "Your fiancé, won't she be worried about you?"

"Wyles, I just couldn't do it. When he didn't come down for breakfast ... and I found him like that ... I just couldn't. I alerted the staff, but as people started to fill the house and the doctor came, and Lady Judith ... I just couldn't stay. How am I to live without my father?"

The sorrow evident in his eyes sparked memories of her own grieving.

"I do know what you mean. My father has been in the ground less than a fortnight, and I feel as if he left only yesterday. At times, I feel as if I can't breathe. I don't know how I'm going to get through today, much less tomorrow ... or even longer. So yes, I do know what you mean. You will manage, though. You will. You have a lovely estate to return to and a beautiful bride. In time, you will find the strength to carry on, for yourself and for her."

"Would you be surprised if I told you I do not love her?" Lord Adrian asked. The words shocked her, and she struggled to respond, but he was the first to speak. "Lord Jameston made that arrangement with my father the day after

Lady Judith was born. He paid handsomely for it as a matter of fact. My father, always the businessman, was unable to turn him down. I was engaged to be married before I could walk." Lord Adrian stood up and began pacing the room.

"As we got older, our fathers would arrange meetings for Lady Judith and I. Horseback riding sessions, dinners, and the like. You would have thought we were royalty, the way we were wined and dined. As if Lord Jameston were trying to build an alliance. He has since admitted he was worried about letting an outsider into his family. Since he and my father go way back, he felt it was fitting.

"So, what do I get? I get the grand estate, and to marry Lady Judith, who I am convinced, does not love me either," he finished.

"Oh, but she does!" Wylie blurted out.

"If you're referring to her little outburst yesterday, I can assure you, that was not out of love. That was because Lady Judith has a flair for the dramatic. She and I had a little chat after you left. She is my fiancé, but you are my friend." At the word friend, he stopped his pacing to stare directly at her, then with complete disregard for what was proper and right, he sat next to her on the settee again. Taking her hand in his. "Oh, if only you were my betrothed. I would be a happy man indeed."

Wylie's heart was racing faster than a fleet of airships. *How can I do what is right, when he has come here uninvited and is doing and saying whatever he damn well pleases?* She jumped up, "Why Lord Adrian, if I had done what you just did, I would be sent to the gallows. How dare you come to my home, proclaiming your feelings for me, the day… the very day your father has died? It just isn't proper!"

He stood up and walked toward her, "Dearest Wylie, I of all people know what is proper and improper. What is right, and what is not right. That is why I had to do it. I had to come; I had to tell you how I truly feel before I say my vows to Judith."

"But Judith! What will she think? What will she do?"

"Judith already knows I don't love her. We know that ours is a marriage of convenience and nothing more."

"Then, why do it? Why enter a loveless marriage if neither of you wants it?"

Lord Adrian sighed heavily, "Because, doing what is right and proper means we often have to do things we don't want to do, for the better of all of those around us." He stood very closely to her again. "Wylie, this may be our only chance, while it is still somewhat proper to do such a thing. May I..." he sucked in a deep breath, "May I embrace you, just this once?"

Wylie stood to her feet, aware of what he was asking, aware what it would mean for her foolish, emotion-driven heart, and stepped toward him.

"Damn you, Adrian."

He placed his gloved hands on her waist and pulled her close. Wylie was very aware that because she was not wearing a corset, nor was he hindered by layers of vests and proper attire, the act of the embrace became something quite intimate. Never before had she been touched by a man, and she was positive if he were not holding her, that she would simply float away.

She dared to lay her head upon his chest, her hands following suit, and they stood together that way for some time. Neither moved nor dared speak for fear of destroying the moment. It would never happen again, she was sure of it. After today, after this brief moment in time ... Lord Adrian would marry her former best friend, and she would only be the poor stable girl and a vague memory.

Time stood still for them, and as their legs grew tired of standing, they finally stepped away from each other. Lord Adrian took her hand in his and placed the softest of kisses upon her fingertips.

"My beloved," he whispered the words tenderly. She knew it was his goodbye. From that moment on, they were once more employer and stable hand. It had to be that way because that's what was right. His eyes reddened, and he turned abruptly and exited her humble abode. The door remained part way open, but she didn't move for what felt like forever, not until the sound of Chaos' hoof beats faded in the distance.

"Goodbye, my beloved Adrian." They'd had a brief twinkling, like when a star shone its brightest before it burned out. It was more than she dared hope for, to find out he felt the same way. It was something she would treasure forever. If she never found love again, at least she had tasted it for one ephemeral moment.

Wylie felt a renewed impulse to help the people of Lugwallow fight for what was theirs. If the Vicar had not shared what was to happen in the future, she could at least do them that service. It was most urgent that the people know what was in store them.

CHAPTER SIX

Wylie pulled her corset over her chemise and laced it up good and tight. Unsure how much time had been lost by Lord Adrian's visit, she hoped to visit most of the residents of Lugwallow before rushing to Dobbinsturn to attend to her stable chores. The mysterious pocket watch device would have to wait 'til another day.

Once Wylie had donned her dress, she grabbed her only other pair of boots. Trimmed with leather and usually only brought out if she was attending church, these boots were beginning to show their age as well. She looked longingly at her comfortable, but manure-stained Wellingtons and wished this were such an occasion that would allow for her to wear them.

This is no time to get weak, Wylie. She checked herself in the mirror. It was a rare thing for Wylie to wear a dress, and she knew even her neighbors would be taken aback. Perhaps the extra attention to her appearance would alert them to the importance of the situation, and they would take her more seriously.

Wylie looked longingly at her goggles, knowing they wouldn't fit over her up-style hairdo and that she would have no need for them today. She would not leave her house without her satchel, however, and that she secured around her waist, placing her father's odd device inside. She knew just where to start in Lugwallow; surely the nosy widow Turpin had seen Lord Adrian leave well beyond the time that was proper for an unwed lady in the poorest parish in London. Wylie decided it was best to squelch the rumors sure to come from the woman's mouth, should she happen to speak to anyone besides her aging son who lived with her. She shut the door to her house and walked the short distance to the Turpin home.

Knocking roughly, Wylie noticed all the grooves and knots in the battered old door. The brass had long ago become discolored and was in desperate need of replacement, and the hinges had been redone a time or two already, but it was obvious they were in need of repair as well. The door creaked open, and the large woman behind it warily poked her head out.

"Afternoon dearie, what brings you to call?"

"Mrs. Turpin, I'm afraid I have some terrible news."

"Oh! Is that why that dashing young man spent time in your home unattended this day?"

"No, Mrs. Turpin, that was my employer, and I am afraid he has very little to do with what I need to tell you." The look on the widow Turpin's face was one of such disappointment that Wylie almost giggled, but managed to stifle her laughter.

"Mrs. Turpin, I have recently been informed that Lord Jameston of Dobbinsturn Parish has joined with two other investors to buy Lugwallow from the Vicar and force us all out on the streets. I don't know when he is coming, but we must warn everyone. We must give our neighbors and friends a chance to get out while they can still salvage their belongings." The widow stared at her in disbelief. "Either that or we must find a way to stop him."

The widow Turpin let out an audible gasp, so loud and edged with dramatics that Wylie was sure she would simply fall over from a heart attack.

"Wylie my dear, I have been here a great many years, and I can assure you if anyone takes my home from me it will be over my dead body." The woman's large frame supported a heavy bosom which heaved up and down alarmingly the angrier she became.

"Then, Mrs. Turpin, surely there is something we can do to prevent such an attack on our livelihood." Wylie responded.

"This house as with many of the homes here were purchased many years ago by Thomas Wilfred Fleming's father. I remember it well. I was a child when my parents moved here though we had lost some of our family to the black plague. Thomas's father was invigorating to listen to, he gave us hope of a better life." Mrs. Turpin paused to wipe away a year. "When he first purchased this parish and built the new church it was a very exciting time. Dobbinsturn was a bustling city of enchantment with much to offer those who could afford it, but Lugwallow was supposed to be that for us, small as it is, it was a parish of dreams for the poor." She paused again, her expression one of deep reminiscence.

"I don't even know how it got to be the blight that it is, I suppose Thomas had planned to keep it up, but at his age, he can't afford the repairs. Time and elements are harsh. I always assumed when he passed that his son would do right by him and fix it up. However, if he is looking to sell, then I supposed that is not to be." Nettie Turpin walked over to the window, and stared out onto the street, her head lifting to take in the skies.

"When I was a child, it was a wonderful time to live here. The airships had not yet taken over the skies, and the streets were not so crowded. I often played outside as a child and once had the great honor of meeting the Queen as she passed through, though I doubt if I was more than four or five years of age at the time."

"As the youngest of six children, you can imagine my mother and father barely had two shillings to rub together when we moved here, but we were happy. My father obtained work, and things got better for us after that until my brother caught the consumption. The little we had saved went to trying to save him."

"He died shortly after that, and my mother soon followed suit. Then it was just the five of us children. My father left this house to my youngest brother, and when he left home years ago to seek his fortune, he, in turn, left it to my eldest sister. When she married and moved in with her husband, she had no further use for it. We have all lost touch over the years, but this house is all I have left of my family." By the time she had finished her story, a stream of steady tears had rolled over her wrinkled, well-rounded face. She didn't speak for a long time, and the lump in the back of Wylie's throat threatened to let loose a dam of tears that Wylie had been clinging to.

"You know what, my dear? I'll be goldarned if some wealthy crook is going to take this away from me!" Wylie's face erupted in a smile, the widow had responded better than she had hoped.

"Then surely, Ms. Turpin, we can band together and give the Vicar enough money that he doesn't just give up our homes to someone who would wish us harm. I mean, surely the law will not allow for a man, even a man with money, to take away what is not rightfully his? Surely the Vicar will see that the sale of our homes will put us all out on the streets with nowhere to go?"

Nettie Turpin nodded her head. "More than that, my dear, we are all descendants, brothers, and sisters of the original tenants. Rightfully, Lugwallow belongs to us, crumbling structures and all, we should have some say in the sale!" she huffed, placing her hands on her wide hips.

"Will you speak to the people, Nettie? I am afraid I haven't as much pull around here as you." Wylie was formulating a plan but needed to escape to Dobbinsturn to put it into action.

"You bet your arse I will." In an uncharacteristic move, Wylie stepped forward and hugged the widow. She nodded to the widow's middle-aged son, who hadn't spoken a word from the moment she had entered the house.

"Thank you, Nettie. I have an idea, but I'll need to go over to Dobbinsturn Parish today. I shall return as soon as I can. Hopefully, we still have a little time before they take action."

"Yes, m'dear. We must not lose hope yet. Go! Do what you must, I'll talk to the people." With that, Nettie was rushing her out the door. Internally Wylie rejoiced that the widow would be taking over the news sharing responsibilities. She had been living a somewhat solitary lifestyle, even more so now that her father was gone. She enjoyed tending Lord Adrian's horses, but her enjoyment of the animals may not have been entirely altruistic, as she now knew without a doubt that it was her adoration of Lord Adrian that made her workdays so enjoyable.

She rushed back home to change out of the dress which left her feeling a bit exposed, and uncomfortable. *Thank God, I didn't have to go around town in this thing.* It may have been looked down upon for a woman to wear trousers, but she was no society woman and she would do as she damn well pleased. After changing and pulling on the comfort of her manure-covered Wellingtons, she was on her way to Dobbinsturn moving as quickly as possible.

If only she had thought to ask Adrian to recommend a trustworthy clockmaker. *Too late for that, Wylie.* She would just have to take her chances on the streets of Dobbinsturn and hope Lady Luck was on her side.

CHAPTER SEVEN

Wylie was well aware of the stares that followed her as she hurried along. She kept her eyes focused downward to avoid making eye-contact with anyone. She purposely crossed to the other side of the street to keep from passing Dobbinsturn's well-known brothel, *The Tainted Lady*. No clever disguise in the name, no trying to hide what went on behind its mahogany doors. The sound of raucous laughter from within the building crawled up Wylie's spine like a parasite. It seemed to whisper to her subconscious: this is where you'll end up if you don't stop Lord Jameston.

Wylie quickened her steps, her eyes darting this way and that in the hopes of finding a clockmaker. She had passed one on her way in, but aware that she was still in the parish of Lugwallow, decided against taking any chances. Then, just up ahead, the sun glinted off a sign.

The Handy Ticker.

Well, that seems promising enough. She had to cross the street again, but since she was well past the brothel, she took a deep breath and hurried to the door. A rusting faux-gold handle allowed the door to click open under pressure from her fingers. She stepped inside and gasped. Such an array of clocks and watches and clock faces. The sounds of simultaneous ticking was overwhelming as she entered the tiny but well-kept store.

"Hello?" she inquired pleasantly. Though she didn't see anyone immediately, her eyes fell on a case of polished, second-hand pocket watches. She stepped closer to them, admiring the lovely images of fairies, trains, and other themes that adorned the cases. None of them looked like the item she carried in her utility belt pocket.

"May I help you, miss?" An elderly gentleman emerged from a narrow doorway, wiping oil from his fingers with a tattered brown rag. He gave her a stern up and down look before coming from behind the counter to face her.

"Yes, um..." Worried that the gentleman would assume she had stolen the rare item, she glanced down at the case. "I was looking for a special pocket watch." The word 'special' caused his eyebrows to arch.

"Don't think we carry anything particularly 'special' here, miss.

"Sir, you misunderstand. My father ... He had a special watch ... perhaps an heirloom, I'm not sure."

"Did you break it, lass? I can certainly try to fix it, it would be cheaper than replacing it." She felt her heart racing faster, fear welling in the back of her throat. If he thought she was a thief or if he tried to take it from her, there was nothing she could do.

"Well no, not exactly. I have it. I just wanted to know more about it, what it might be worth. My father passed recently, and it's all I have left that was his." The shopkeeper studied her face, his elderly wrinkled face crinkling at the corners of his mouth as he smiled at her.

"Well, let's see what we can find out, lass. I'm not going to take it from you if that's what 'yer 'fraid of. I've more than my share of clocks and pocket watches… more than I know what ta' do with." Still, she hesitated to reach into her utility pocket. "Miss, if ya need help, I may be one of the few around here you can trust." He stood only a couple of inches under her five foot five. He looked harmless enough, and she reckoned she would be able to deal with him if he tried anything.

Moving slowly, Wylie unlatched the flap on the pouch at her hip and pulled out the pocket watch. She hadn't taken the time to study it in the daylight, and now she saw that she was right to be worried about it being taken from her. Such exquisite details on the bronze dragon that adorned the front, it nearly took her breath away. So shocked was she by its ethereal beauty that she dropped it, and it hit the floor with a resounding thud. Afraid she had broken it, she hurriedly picked it up and was relieved to see it was still in one piece. The heavy bronze metal case seemed sturdy enough to withstand rough treatment.

The dragon's eyes on the face were made of impeccably cut rubies. Tiny green emeralds adorned the tips of the wings, and traces of gold outlined every groove. It was the most glorious item she had ever held in her hands, and she clung to it fiercely, afraid to place it on the counter; afraid the shop keeper would see its value and take it from her.

"Well, let's have a look, shall we?"

She stood paralyzed, unable to move or speak.

"Well?"

She glanced toward the door, wondering if it would be best for her to run out of the shop right then and there.

"You're a bit skittish, aren't you lass?" It was now or never, she didn't even think, as she thrust the exquisite item onto the counter. She kept her eyes on the pocket watch hardly daring to blink, half expecting the watchmaker to scarper at any moment.

"Hmmm," he said, "Interesting ... lovely ... oh my ... Simply delightful!" He continued, praising the thing, as he studied it through various lenses attached to his goggles. "Well, miss, I can see why you were skittish, but I assure you have nothing to fear from me. However, I would not leave this shop without hiding this securely." She nodded her head up and down. He went back to examining it, finally popping it open. His eyes opened wide in surprise when the wings unfolded. He stared in fascination, just as she had, at the moon and star face that took the place of a normal timepiece. She watched as he fiddled with the small brass knob at the top.

The wonderment that shone from his eyes was like a child playing with a new toy for the first time. She heard the gentle whirring as the small gear lifted mechanically from the wings.

"Curious." The flat gear had taken its place over particular points of the dragon that was contained inside the moon face. He gently closed the device and handed it back to her. "Well, my dear. That is certainly no pocket watch."

"Then you know what it is?"

He shook his head at her question. "I'm afraid I don't, lass. Listen to me, you were right to want to know its worth, but I would discourage you from trying to sell it. It's very rare I see such workmanship anymore. It seems a waste to trade for something as temporary as money. You say it was your father's?"

She nodded.

"Don't give it up …" He paused, an unspoken question hanging in the air.

"Uh … Wylie sir, my name is Wylie Petford. My father was Nicholas Petford." She stuck out her hand. His face crinkled as he took her hand in his, lips turned up in a friendly smile. She hadn't known her grandfather, but she decided that he would have been much like this man. Kindness and hard work etched into his face.

"Name is Piercy. Piercy Webster. Clockmaker, gadget-lover, and trustworthy as they come."

She smiled back at him, glad that she had made the right choice to show him the item.

"Well, Mr. Webster, it's a pleasure to make your acquaintance. I've yet to decide if I will sell it or not. Please, can you tell me what it might be worth?"

"Fraid I can't, lass. Seeing as how I don't know what it is. If you ask me, it's still a pocket watch in some respects. I'd say, however, that it's a watch for the stars. It leads up to something, I can see that. Though I don't know what that something is, don't know if 'ya noticed, but all the dots on the gear mechanism lined up perfectly with the dragon inside the glass face."

She nodded again. "I did notice that, what do you think it means?"

"Well, now that ... that I don't know. Can't even speculate about what it could be."

"Well, what do you think I should do?"

"That's a good question, give me a moment to think. Ah! I know just the man."

"You do?" she responded.

"Yes, a good friend of mine. Trustworthy, honest. Last of his kind really, owns a shop over towards Kinnemore. You'll want to wait until tomorrow to go, as it's getting late. A young lass like yourself shouldn't be on the streets at night."

"I understand, but I'm afraid my well-being, as well as the well-being of many others, is at stake. I must figure something out as quickly as possible. If I am not able to sell it, Lugwallow may be in trouble." She expected him to ask questions, but he merely mumbled something and pulled out a bit of thin parchment to write on.

"Here, the man I'm sending you to, he's an inventor of sorts. He knows everything about everything. You're gonna exit my shop, and head left down Hertfordshire, you keep on until you reach Windmill Ave., take a right on Windmill. You know Windmill can go on forever, so make sure you pay close attention. You're going to make a left on Auburn, and his shop is right there. If anyone can help you, he can. He's a bit mad, but don't hold that against him. The man lost his wife and daughters to a sudden illness. He's holed himself away in his shop ever since. He's the only one I know that won't try to lay a finger on ya' or steal this out of your cold dead hands. Keep it close, ya hear me?"

She nodded again.

"Another thing, lass, you're gonna need this." He reached under the counter and pulled out a beat-up old derringer. "She may be old, but she's still got a bit o' fight left in the ol' girl." He shoved the gun in a leather holster and handed it to her. "Take good care of her, won't ya?"

"Mr. Webster... I can't take this! I have no money." He put his hand up to stop her.

"Now I don't recall asking for payment, but if yer worried about that, you can stop by again and let me know yer alive. Tell me if ya found out anything about that odd contraption, eh?"

She nodded her head vigorously. "What about you? Don't you need to protect yourself?"

"No worries, lass. I have my trusty old flintlock. Darn thing has been with me more years than I can remember." He pulled it from beneath the counter as if to reassure her. "I'll be all right. Now, you git. Don't forget to step back in and say hello, ya understand?"

With a smile that lit up her face, she thanked him again, grabbed the paper, and followed the route that he had laid out for her.

He had even marked in some of the shop names and a couple of statues so she could keep better track of where she was. At the top of the page he had written a name:

Dr. Hubert Mullings, Scientist, and on the map he had written out the name of the shop, The Dusty Gadget, and marked it with an arrow.

Oh heavens. I still have the chores to do at the stables. I'd better go do that now, and maybe I'll have time to visit Dr. Mullings after that. Wylie glanced up at the clock over Mr. Webster's shop. It's only 10:30, I should have plenty of time.

By the time Wylie had walked across town to Lord Adrian's, she realized she hadn't eaten yet that day and was starving. She made a little side trip to the rear of the mansion and knocked on the kitchen door. Nora, the cook, was one of the few staff in Lord Adrian's employ who actually liked Wylie.

"You just come on in and set yourself down, girl," said Nora. "I've got just the thing for a hungry young lady."

In no time, Wylie was spooning up steaming hot onion soup and stuffing down great slabs of fresh buttered bread. "You're a marvelous cook, Nora. This is food fit for a king."

"Ah, get away with ya. It's just plain fare, but it will fill that empty spot, sure enough." The grin on her face did little to hide her pleasure at the compliment.

It took much longer to complete the stable chores than Wylie had anticipated, so by the time she was done it was already late afternoon. She debated whether to put off her visit to Dr. Mullins 'til the next day, but then remembered the pocket watch and how anxious she was to learn more about it.

Dobbinsturn was three times as large as Lugwallow, her destination was almost to Kinnemore so that it was already dark when she arrived in front of The Dusty Gadget. Through the front window she was able to see one lighted lamp which seemed to be the only sign of activity in the place.

Oh, dear. What was I thinking, coming here so late in the day? A lone carriage rolled by, the driver tipping his hat to her. She nodded back, looking around for anyone who might be of help. To her dismay, she was nearly alone. A tall man with a large top hat walked by, and not to be mistaken for a lady of the night, she bit her lip, looked to the ground, and didn't say a word. The chill of the evening was gradually creeping in, so she finally got up her nerve and knocked on the door. No answer.

"I should've known that," she said aloud, as she tried the latch, pleased to find it unlocked, and stepped inside, closing the door behind her. "Stupid girl," she cursed herself. "What do you think you're doing?"

"Yes, what indeed?" A man appeared quite suddenly holding a lamp. His face was illuminated by its gentle glow, which made him seem almost ghostly, and she tripped over her words.

"Oh dear me… oh, heavens. You must be the Hubert… er… Scientist doctor. Er…. Dr. Hubert Mullings, Scientist." She was shaking so badly from nerves and cold, she could barely speak properly.

"Yes, I am Dr. Mullings. How did you hear of me?" His voice softened to low tones, and for whatever reason, possibly her overactive imagination, she felt suddenly afraid.

"Mr. Webster sent me. He said you were a good friend and that you would be able to help me. He promised me that you were a good man," she added, almost as if placing blame on Mr. Webster if Dr. Mullings turned out to be anything but.

At the mention of Mr. Webster's name, the doctors faced softened instantaneously.

"Mr. Webster? Still alive after all this time?" he laughed a hearty laugh. "That man was like a father to me, growing up." She watched with interest as he seemed to retreat somewhere far off into his memories.

"Indeed, I'm sure he was. He spoke very highly of you. So, I must ask… would you be willing to help me?"

He didn't respond immediately, but instead turned away from her and walked back towards the shadows of his gadget shop. The lamplight wasn't bright enough to see what he was doing, the moonlight through the windows too dim to see more than a few feet in front of her.

"Dr. Mullings?" her voice trembling. Never one to be intimidated, she took a step forward, but the sound of feet walking about stopped her suddenly. Realizing she knew nothing of this man, she froze on the spot, hoping against hope that the man would do her the courtesy of answering. It felt like every second the shop grew darker, and her fears grew along with it. She could hear sounds and some movement where he was but resolved not to call out again. Obviously, he was busy, and she found herself moving backward toward the entrance.

A fast getaway seemed to be her best recourse at the moment. It was night time after all, and she was alone with a strange man. She had been a fool to come here. Another step back, and she would be able to turn and run back out the door from whence she'd come.

At that precise moment, the entire shop lit up. Dr. Mullings stood near a switch on the wall, she almost laughed in relief... He had only retreated to turn on the light! Her nerves started to calm a bit, she could tell he was fussing with something near the light, another lever of sorts? She heard a gently cranking as a sort of tube lowered onto the wall-mounted lantern that so brilliantly lit his shop.

In the next moment, a sprinkling of color erupted above her fiery red hair, and her gaze was immediately drawn to the ceiling.

An array of prismatic colors danced on the ceiling, brilliant hues of red, blue, yellow, and green that caused her to gasp in delight.

Wylie was completely transfixed. Never before had she seen such a dazzling array. She walked towards the lamp on the wall to study it more closely, noticing the elegant glass shade on the base, but seeing nothing else to account for how it gave off such voluminous pigment.

"Dr. Mullings, how did you do that? How do you cause the light to change like that?"

"Don't be silly, m'dear. I didn't cause the light to change." He stuck his hand out to pull a small lever affixed to the wall. Pulling it downward, she heard the sound of pulleys and cranking as the lamplight changed color again. Once again, to her delight, the ceiling erupted in a profusion of gorgeous hues, a mixture of purples and oranges, dancing about like a sort of magic light show. It lit up the doctor's workspace, as well as a variation of doodads and baubles around the shop that were no doubt his inventions in various stages of completion.

"What you see is the effects of what is called a kaleidoscope. Only on a much larger scale. Back when I was a young lad, around 1816, I attended college with a man by the name of Sir David Brewster. A man of passion, he and I hit it off well, in fact, you might say that his little invention was our combined effort. Though most would attribute the invention to him."

"You came in as I was getting it ready for its first test run, but what I'm working on here is integrating the Kaleidoscope for use on modern lamps. I have used Sir Brewster's concept, which is what that tube is on the lamp," he paused to gesture towards it.

"I see. Please, how do you change the colors that emanate on the ceiling?" Her curious mind always wanting to know how things functioned. No doubt a characteristic she had inherited from her father.

"You can't see the bauble at the end of these wires that are connected to this lever, but every time I pull this lever, the small clicking sound you hear, is color disks on a small tray above the lamp which rotates and changes. I realize you can't see the disk tray as it's hidden by the glass shade and kaleidoscope tubing, but that's what makes it so dazzling."

"It may not be as practical as Singer's newfangled sewing machine, but it's not as boring either. While all of London frolics about under white lights, I have taken a step toward the future! Imagine the Queen displaying my light show in her ballroom? It will be extravagant! Extraordinary!" His face lit up with the sparkle of what the future may hold, and for a minute Wylie was able to visualize it. Though she assumed it would be something only the wealthy could afford. She knew she had been given the gift of seeing it with her own eyes and she surely would never forget it. "I see. Well, the whole system is quite marvelous beyond words, Dr. Mullings."

"Are you an inventor?"

She laughed and shook her head. "A maker of things, perhaps, but nowhere near what you're doing here. My father was not an inventor either, though he was good with his hands and he created quite a bit of beautiful furniture and other necessities. Which is why I'm quite perplexed at this…" It was now or never. She reached into her utility pocket and pulled out the device to show him. "This is what I found, in a secret compartment in a dresser my father had built. I don't know what it is, though it looks like a pocket watch. It's the reason I went to visit Mr. Webster today, and why I am here to see you. Do you think you'll be able to help me?"

As she repeated her request for the second time that day, her resolve grew, and her fear lessened. If he couldn't help her, she would search the world over until she found answers or fetched a good price for the gadget.

His eyes widened when he saw it, and gingerly taking it, he turned it over and over in his hands. Inspecting every detail, admiring the diamonds and emeralds and gold filigree. When he opened it, his jaw dropped, and he stood quite still for a moment, just staring at the dragon in the center.

"This is quite the loveliest thing I have ever seen."

"Yes, 'thing' is quite right. Do you not know what it is either? Mr. Webster said it's not a pocket watch." She crossed her arms over her corseted top, diligently watching his every move.

"Yes, well he was right in that respect," he said, coming across as a little out of breath. "It's quite magnificent. It looks like a constellation finder or some sort of dragon summoning device. Of course, that's silly, though."

Dragon Summoner? The idea made her giggle, and he cast her an irritated glance.

"I was just merely stating what it looked like. I wasn't saying that's what it is."

Oh, he's a bit mad. That's for sure.

"Here, take this," he placed it back in her hand and turned his back to her again. This time, she was able to watch his every move since his system of lights lit up the little gadget shop like a palace parade. He retrieved a book from a shelf full of books, and set it down on his worktable, flipping quickly through the pages. Not finding what he was looking for, he grabbed another.

That book didn't have what he needed either, and soon he was surrounded by books of all shapes and sizes. Passing over several more, Dr. Mullins ran his hand over their spines before he finally grabbed a rather worn leather-bound tome. It was larger than a normal size book with leather straps bundling it closed.

She had never seen its equal, and it was her turn to be shocked into silence. He shoved several volumes out of the way and lay it down, unlatching the buckles and pulling out a piece of paper from the beginning of it that had been neatly folded and tucked inside the cover. He beckoned her to come over to him, and she complied. "Read this. I don't care how long it takes you." His eyes had taken on a crazed, half-cocked stare.

His tone was more than just insistent, so not wanting to risk pushing him over the edge, she simply responded with a polite, "Yes, of course." She stood next to him, pulling the book closer, as he walked away, disappearing into a back room.

Her heart now beating rapidly, she worried about what she would find in its pages. As she opened it, the first rough page had nothing on it but a hand-written inscription.

DRAGALETH

Said to be a myth, Dragaleth refers to the race of dragons who are in charge of the balance of good and evil on Earth. The Dragaleth is a combination of two dragons, one of the order of Teselym and the other of Siapheg. Teselym protects humanity from evil and executes justice when necessary. The Teselym enacts the balance of good. Siapheg brings evil and ensures that humanity will never be entirely free from the sadness of death, betrayal, and lies.

The Dragaleth are said to be controlled by the gods, but their existence has never been historically proven. The story of Dragaleth surfaced in the 1400s when a lone survivor of a ship carrying the black plague wrote his personal account of the events leading up to the darkest age in history.

Perplexed, she flipped to the first page. An illustration there stopped her in her tracks. She knew now she needed to do as the Doctor had asked and read what was inside. There was no turning back now.

CHAPTER EIGHT

I, Thaddeus McCollum, being of sound mind, but not of sound body, do hereby state the following is the truth, to the best of my memory.

As an adult born and raised on the water, I had only known the seas when the Black Death hit my family's ship. The boils and puss and the smell of death were something that to this day, on my death bed, I have been unable to wipe from my memory.

My mother would often retell the stories told to her of the time known as the Crusades, which started in the 11th century. The very first crusade was merely a cry for help from Pope Urban II to stop the spread of alternate religion, it sparked a series of crusades which the church demanded its followers support if they wished to be absolved of their sins and guaranteed a place in heaven.

This crusade sparked the evil of men's hearts, and soon it became clear to my grandparents that the Church wanted to suppress any opposition whatsoever. They, or at least the men at the head of the church, wanted to have full control. The evil they perpetrated ended thousands of innocent lives. None were spared, not men, women, or children. My grandparents, fearing for their lives, took their meager savings and my mother and left their home.

Mother was a baby when her parents took her to sea with a small crew of friends and relatives in 1282. Aboard a large sailing transport known as an Usciere, with not much room for any extra crew, my grandparents agreed to help care for the ship's horses and muck out the stables. With the crusades on the rise, horses proved to be a desperate need that would not go away. All one had to do was to follow the route of the Crusades, and they would know where the next slew of horses was required. This was something the captain was very good at.

After nearly a decade on the sea, my mother became old enough to join the crew and help care for the horses as well. It was during that time she remembers the night she saw the dragons rise. With no name for them at that moment, my mother referred to them as winged beasts.

The skies had opened in a deluge of rain, much to the crew's delight, as water supplies were running low. The downpour would mean water for the horses and people aboard. As it stormed that evening, my mother stole out of her parent's cabin and onto the starboard deck to look at the thundering skies as she huddled under the cover of a lifeboat to keep dry.

Not long after, in the darkness, she saw the winged beasts for the first time. One as black as the night from whence it came, its horns like those of a Viking helmet. The other beast was of pure opalescent white. She compared the loveliness of it to an angel that embodied heaven itself. Suddenly it was as if the Earth had been rent in two, for the storm that followed their rising, was one like she had never seen. It woke everyone onboard though they didn't see the beasts, and the ship nearly went under the waves more than once.

My mother spent the next few days questioning friends and family about the strange creatures, but oddly, she had been the only one to see them. She soon came to believe they had been a hallucination due to her exhaustion and the storm.

When they docked in port at Lisbon, Portugal to gather supplies and pick up another shipment of horses, my mother casually brought up the topic of the strange creatures to shopkeepers and children alike. No one seemed able to confirm her vision, and fearing she would be declared unstable and separated from her family, she tucked the vision of the scaled monsters away.

They sailed from port that night to deliver the horses they had obtained to Acre, Israel where another Crusade was underway. However, demand was so high, they immediately sailed back to Spain to retrieve another herd.

The seas were rough, often causing injuries or illness. They were delayed several days because of it, and by the time they had retrieved an additional fifty horses from Spain and sailed back to deliver them in Israel, the final Crusade was over.

While the captain and crew haggled to sell off the herd, the ship remained anchored in Acre for some time. My mother played with a group of children near the harbor most days.

The children acted out a story that involved a great white beast they called a dragon that had flown in aid of Al-Ashraf Khalil in his crusade against Acre two years before. They swore it was the dragon who helped Al-Ashraf win the battle and put a stop to the crusades once and for all. Though it had taken quite some time, there was now peace. The white dragon had disappeared afterward, and the survivors had come together to clean up the bodies and restore the city.

When my mother asked them to describe the dragon, they told her in detail about the great winged beast, which she knew to be identical to the one she had seen nearly three years beforehand. When she boarded the ship several nights later with her family and the remaining twenty-five horses, my mother knew she would not sleep until she had learned more about the dragon that had helped to bring an end to the Crusades in 1291.

Though the Crusades had ended, the fighting and battles had not, and there was always a need to sail somewhere or other to deliver more livestock. At times, they would pick up a herd of cattle and use them for trade and barter.

My mother and father, having grown up aboard the ship, fell in love when they were but seventeen and nineteen. They married a year later, and after two miscarriages, my mother gave birth to me in 1305. That's when my parents decided to leave the ship and build a life for us on solid land. The captain, having aged and ready to pass the ship off to his son, gave them a bit of coin for their time and hard work to help them get established ashore.

They traveled from place to place, stopping wherever my mother found work as a seamstress and my father could get employment at ship building or fishing. Finally, we ended up along the Thames near the port of London and father gained an apprenticeship in the shop of a blacksmith, where he earned and saved enough coin to set himself up in a little shop of his own.

As I came of age, my mother taught me to sew and read and write. My father taught me to forge metal and hammer down iron. My mother told me about the dragons, and though I believed it to be a fairy tale, I never grew tired of hearing the story, even as an adult. When I was old enough to work, my parents thought it best to return to the sea.

By that time, my father's blacksmith trade had grown, and they had acquired a little home for themselves through shrewdness and a lot of ingenuity. They were able to sell their home, at a fair profit, as the economy seemed to be on the rise despite the outbreak of the black plague.

It never seemed to stop the ships from docking, and the port never slept as many sailing vessels came and went. Living there was exciting for me, as I learned how to make various weapons and tools, but I knew my parents craved the peace and quiet of the sea. Greed was on the rise, and the exchange of money increased at a frenetic pace, causing everything to rise rapidly in cost.

About the time the house was sold, father met a ship owner who was cash-strapped. His ship, a cog called Katarina, was bearing a load of tea from China and had been caught in a devastating storm, so violent it blew off the hatch covers, and though the ship received minimal damage, the entire cargo was ruined from salt water entering the hold and soaking the tea.

The man's misfortune was my father's gain, and he purchased the ship that very day. The night we left the Port of London, I sat in the stern watching the sky. It was that very evening, I saw what my mother had so often told me of. Two mighty dragons flew across the moon, and I watched them as they descended upon the city we had just left. My mother's quest now became my own.

Aboard the new ship, I worked as a cabin boy as my parents sailed from England to Spain, to Ireland and back again. They traded and bartered whatever promised to make a reasonable profit. We didn't have much room for horses and could barely manage the three to five we kept aboard when we were able. We dealt mostly in tea and spices, and my mother proved to have a knack for trading. How we managed, I'll never know but the small crew and I never went hungry.

I spent all my free time learning about navigation and seamanship. I had enjoyed our time on land and still took advantage of occasional opportunities while in port, but was still curious about the dragons, and the more I learned, the more I wanted to know. I grabbed hold of every book I could get my hands on in the hopes of finding out more about the creatures. Finally, one day it was in a tiny curiosity shop that I stumbled on a journal by a Captain Daniel Bloggart.

It was like finding gold. The book told of the crusades, and how the gods, heartbroken over men's evil ways, had cried real tears. Their tears fell upon the Earth and awoke a magic so long asleep that no one could have predicted what would happen. The very day the gods wept, two great dragons rose into the sky.

Captain Bloggart went on to describe the dragon's purpose in the course of human events, but still, without further validation, I didn't know how much of it was true. Two shillings seemed a little steep, but I didn't bother to haggle and would have paid twice the price as the journal contained so much pertinent information. Of course, most of the information remains unverified and its creator unknown to me.

The night my world changed for the worse, I was forty-six years of age. I had spent most of my life trying to find out more about the beasts while I took care of my aging mother who had grown ill at the time. As I kept the night watch, my eyes beheld the dragons once more -- it was the moment I had waited for my entire life.

The beasts had come back. This time, they were locked in a power struggle, like a mid-air dance. The crew had long since gone to sleep, so I stood there with my hand on the helm watching the beasts dart this way and that. At one point they came so close to the ship I thought they would rip the sails clean off.

I couldn't look away, nor run to safety. I was transfixed. They belched fire and tackled one another, often becoming so entangled they fell into the sea. Then they would rise up again and continue fighting well into the night. Just as the sun began to peek over the horizon, the white one flew over the ship, the black one chased after it laboriously as they were both tired from battle. The white dragon took one furious swipe at the black dragon and knocked it out of the sky.

I watched the huge black body fall into the sea, its tail striking the port side of the ship, and then the black dragon gradually sank out of sight. The white dragon flew off into the rising sun, and that was the last of it. Or so I thought. I hadn't yet had time to read the entirety of the journal I had found, and I wouldn't for some time.

That was the day the Black Death came upon us. I had longed to return to land, as life at sea was losing its attraction. My mother was one of the first to fall ill. She died quickly, as did others and we wasted no time in relinquishing the bodies to the deeps. The plague traveled so swiftly through the crew I was sure I would never see land again. By the time I finally did, my father had died as well, and there was only a handful of us left.

The day came when I was sailing the ship alone, and a poor job I was doing of it. The only other person alive was the cook's helper, and he was failing fast. I was now desperate to get ashore but knew if I tried to make port I would be refused entry due to the death and pestilence onboard.

When the cook's helper had taken his last breath, I sent him to his resting place in the deeps and then I devised a plan. I knew if I could get to London, I would have a good chance of finding work and making a life for myself on shore. I also knew I would never be able to sail the ship up the River Thames on my own.

I had learned enough about navigation to know I wasn't far from the mouth of the English Channel. As long as I was in the Channel, I would be fine. Only when I tried to land would I be open to inspection.

Therefore, I timed my arrival along the south coast of England for the middle of the night. Thankfully, there was a full moon, and I was able to watch the shore for a low beach area with no lights nearby. When I found such a spot, I steered directly for it and grounded her.

Strapping a purse around my waist with all the money I had been able to find on the ship, and taking a canteen of water and some hard tack, I struck off inland under cover of night and put as much distance as possible between me and the ship. Come daylight I begged rides from passing farm wagons and produce carts until I finally arrived at the outskirts of London.

I quickly found a job as a blacksmith in Dobbinsturn with a man by the name of Cornelius Porter. My father had taught me well, and I advanced quickly with accompanying raises in pay. He was a skilled craftsman and a fair employer. Not many people would have taken a second look at me, being rather weather beaten from my years at sea, but it seemed Lady Luck was on my side for once.

After working with Cornelius that first day, he pointed me toward McCollum Inn, one of the only places in town that was open for new boarders. With access to clean water and a breakfast of real homemade biscuits, I couldn't have imagined heaven being any finer.

Until Mr. Charles McCollum's daughter stepped into the room.

I had a mouth full of food and must have looked a fool staring at her the way I did, but I was sure that she was an angel, with her soft curls of yellow hair that embraced a face full of freckles. She smiled shyly at me while grabbing her breakfast and then retreating from the room.

From then on every time I spotted her I gave her a wide smile, but it would be a good six months before I would finally gather the nerve to say hello.

Most ladies would have thought it improper, but we had stolen enough glances to strike up a conversation.

I continued to work hard, putting all I had into being the best blacksmith I was capable of. At night, after coming home and cleaning up before supper, Elizabeth and I would occasionally steal away to the drawing room of the inn. There were always people about, so it's not as if we were so improper as to be alone, but I found myself drawn to her gentle mannerisms and quiet intellect.

She may have been a woman, but she had a love of Chaucer and all forms of poetry. I fell in love and, nearly eight months later, I purchased a small bit of silver and hand forged a ring for Elizabeth. I professed my love to her in the drawing room where most of our conversations had taken place, and she accepted my hand in marriage.

Meanwhile, the blacksmith shop I worked at had begun to grow. Word had spread about the quality of our work. Old man Porter passed away not long after, and he left the shop to me in his will. I eventually took on more help as well as a business partner, growing the shop into a profitable trade over the next couple of years.

Elizabeth being ten years younger than I gave me two strong sons, and Mr. Charles McCollum insisted I take on their family name. I had nothing to prove my own lineage as I had been born at sea and both my parents were now dead.

Mr. McCollum had been assisting a local physician for several years and studying the healing arts. By now the locals were calling him Dr. McCollum and his services were much in demand. Whenever he could, Dr. McCollum advised me in building and expanding my blacksmith business in order to make it more profitable.

On my fifty-fourth birthday, I sold my business to my partner and went under Dr. McCollum's full-time employ as a medical assistant as well as aiding with the running of the inn. It allowed Elizabeth more time to raise our boys, and me the opportunity to watch them grow up.

I enjoyed learning from the well-educated Dr. McCollum, but I definitely felt my age at times. The boys loved when I would join them in boisterous play which sometimes tired me out, but they were grand times. As they grew older, and Dr. McCollum's medical practice grew, so did the city. The social classes became more separated than ever, but I found that no one remembered me as the man who'd once been a blacksmith. I was a McCollum, part of a family of medical pioneers.

Using my newfound wealth and status, I gained access to some of the grandest libraries in the world where Dr. McCollum and I studied at every opportunity. At the same time, I found, even more, information concerning dragons.

And now, as an old man, I can confess that I have spent the past four decades learning everything I could about dragons. Through the curiosity shop journal that I finally read in its entirety, through mythology, rare eyewitness accounts, paintings and carvings that dated back long before words were committed to paper. This is everything I have learned about the Dragaleth.

If you are reading this, then I have passed from this world to the next, and I have released my findings of the beasts for any who may wish to peruse my studies.

Signed this seventeenth day of March 1387,

Thaddeus McCollum

The following are notes from Thaddeus's findings.

-According to mythology the Dragaleth have existed since the dawn of man but were not resurrected on Earth until the gods cried tears of real heartbreak.

-1290 My mother spots the Dragaleth while out at sea

-1291 Dragaleths aid Al-Ashraf Khalil who marched against the coastal port of Acre, Israel. It was a mere seven weeks that Acre was under siege before they gave in and ended the crusades.

-1305 I was born

-1317 Dragaleth are spotted in England by me as a small boy.

-Over the course of 1318-1325, the owner of the journal spots them sixteen times.

-1346 I spot the Dragaleth over my boat, in which they battle, and one dies.

-1355 I find mythology speaking of the Dragaleth before the world was created.

It says there are two

One is a race called:

TESELYM

Teselym-Protector of the human race, more power than Siapheg. Executes justice when necessary. The Teselym enacts the balance of good.

SIAPHEG

Siapheg- brings evil and ensures that humanity will never be entirely free from the sadness of death, betrayal, and lies. Less powerful than Teselym. (Maybe he brought the flea that gave my ship the Black Death)

Mythology states that if they were ever to be resurrected in real life that they would be a combination of human and dragon. Mythology also states that more often than not, the gods would use twins to complete this feat and that only one Siapheg and Teselym can be alive at a time. When they are resurrected through the human race, it will pass from father to firstborn, the bond of Dragaleth can be passed between siblings if the first dies too quickly, or from parent to child and back to the parent.

A Dragaleth must remain a Dragaleth for a minimum of ten human years before passing the bond onto another sibling or child unless killed beforehand. The gods determine who carries on the bond if there is more than one eligible family member. When an old Dragaleth dies regardless of the cause, the bond immediately passes onto the next of kin. The Dragaleths do not have to kill each other; the ideal is that they dwell in harmony, and they must only maintain the balance of good and evil. If at any point, the balance dips farther towards good, or farther towards evil, the opposite Dragaleth may challenge his or counter to a battle in Dragon form.

The duel is to the death, and the victor must depart peacefully and maintain the balance of both good and evil until another can be raised up to take the place of the Dragaleth who died. The surviving Dragaleth will know it is time for him or her to take to the skies when they are summoned by their human host.

The human host is only able to summon a Dragaleth when they are of age to understand the balance between good and evil. This will be evidenced when they hold the Dracosinum, and the dragon essence balances perfectly. Its gear lining up with its internal workings, and only on the nights when the moon aligns with the North Star.

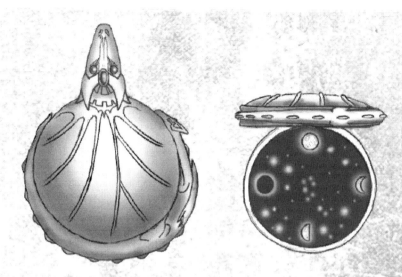

To activate the dragon essence within, the human host must turn the crown of the Dracosinum a total of twelve full turns to the left, and five full turns to the right. This act will unlock the essence of the dragon which will come back to life and make its holder aware if they are ready or not. Once activated, it cannot be undone, and if the human host finds or inherits its Dracosinum and decides not to activate it, the Earth and its people will be left to destroy themselves as the balance of good and evil will eventually run out.

Though I have referred to the possessor of the Dracosinum as a host, make no mistake that the Dragaleth and the human who animates it are one and the same, for it is the essence of the person itself and it has been discovered that one cannot exist without the other. This concludes my findings.

Thaddeus McCullum

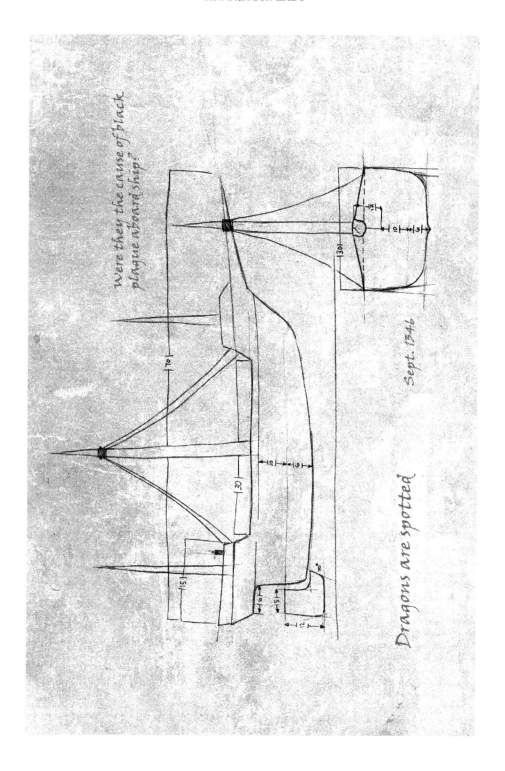

Were they the cause of black plague aboard ship?

Sept. 1346

Dragons are spotted

1096-1099	People's Crusade
1281	My mother born
1282	Mother goes to sea
1290	Dragons are spotted
1291	Last crusade
1294	Mother learns the truth in Acre, Israel
1298-1299	Parent's are in love and marry
1305	I am born
1351	I see dragons with my own eyes, black dragon falls into sea
1353	I get a job as a blacksmith
1355	I marry Elizabeth

CHAPTER NINE

Wylie closed the book and shut her eyes, contemplating everything she had read. She pulled the Dracosinum from her pouch and set it upon the rough wood surface before her. The truth for the moment seemed so far-fetched that she couldn't believe it to be accurate. *Me, a Dragaleth? It's a myth. A fairy tale. It has to be!*

"Did you find out anything?" Dr. Mullins had stayed out of sight until she was done reading. His gruff voice jolted her back to reality.

"I… I…. I need a moment if you please." Picking up the Dracosinum, she walked towards the front of the shop, intent on stepping outside into the night to get a breath of fresh air. But then she thought better of it. Wylie didn't know how the curse worked, but she surely wasn't going to help it along. Instead, she found herself pacing the floor, rolling the ideas around in her mind, like a ship upon the water.

In the meantime, Dr. Mullins took her place at the table and began reading through the information himself. She didn't dare look at him, for fear of what she would see in his face, so instead, she paced back and forth waiting for him to respond to what he read in the worn leather-bound book. He grew very quiet; even his breathing, which had before been heavy, slowed, as he immersed himself in the contents of the book.

When he finished reading, flipping the book this way and that as he studied the drawings, he closed the ancient pages, latched the book closed, and stared at the desktop for a long while, not speaking. Wylie had long since stopped pacing when he finally lifted his eyes from the surface in front of him and turned to face her.

"Miss, may I ask a perfectly serious question?"

She nodded her head in response.

"Have you turned the dial at the top, in the manner in which this book says?" The question caused her breath to catch. What he was asking, what it implied was the very thing she feared. If she performed the action, it would mean stepping from reality into an alternate fantasy in which good and evil dragons, and gods, are real. A situation that Wylie was not sure if she wanted to embrace just yet.

She vigorously shook her head from side to side and purposefully avoided his gaze.

"Well, I can't say that I blame you. I'm not sure if I would be able to, either."

"I'm sorry?" Wylie responded.

"I said, I can't say that I blame you... actuating the balance of good and evil? It's a heavy burden. Please consider one thing though. If you will." She offered him a nod, urging him to go on. "If you are indeed a Dragaleth, and you have a purpose to fulfill, then that means you are one or the other. That also means that your opposite is already roaming the Earth. If you are the Siapheg, then your good counterpart roams freely, unchallenged, and that can't be a terrible thing. However, if you are the Teselym... That means you are the only thing separating death from life, illness from wellness, and deceit from truth. We need you; the people need you. Consider that, before you disregard it completely, eh?"

She couldn't move or think and hardly even breathe at what he was suggesting.

"Please, Dr. Mullins, you don't honestly consider this to be true?" He didn't answer but disappeared into the back room again. When he emerged, he was holding a heavy quilt and pillow.

"Here, please, sleep here tonight. There's a bench just there; you can pull the cushions off and sleep on the floor if you desire. Please don't venture out onto the streets. You have it on my honor, I will not bother you in your sleep. You can leave whenever you like. I just don't want you out on the streets alone; it isn't safe. A man was killed not far from here just a fortnight ago. A good man, a captain."

She nearly choked on her own spittle.

"A fortnight ago?"

"Well, a fortnight and a day. They say he was murdered by some beast, but they've been unable to determine what kind. A large dog, perhaps? No one has seen it."

"That was the night my father passed." She bowed her head, taking the blanket and pillow from the man's hands before retiring to the corner of the shop, where the bench was.

"I'm sorry for your father's passing." He seemed to know something, so much more than what he was saying, but he didn't continue the conversation. Dr. Mullins pulled the lever for his kaleidoscope lighting system down a few notches, which sent the room into near darkness except for the softer light of an oil lamp sitting on the counter, near the books. He left her alone with her thoughts and disappeared into the back room.

Wylie picked her way over to the bench in the dim light and decided to just lie on it, covering herself with the quilt rather than move the cushions onto the floor as he had suggested. Try as she might, she was unable to sleep. The sudden news of the Captain's death screamed loud and long in her mind, making sleep impossible. *If I am going to accept what I read about the Dracosinum as truth, then it's possible that the Teselym and Siapheg exist. As in, this very time… this very century.* She turned over on her other side, her mind reeling. *If the Captain was killed by a beast the very same night my father died, is it really such a leap to think that a Dragaleth killed him? Is that why the beast has never been found?*

She turned the Dracosinum over in her hands, running her fingers over the cool bronze of the dragon wings on the outside. *Am I really considering that my father was a Dragaleth? What if he just had the Dracosinum because it was passed down to him? Except the very night he died, a man was murdered?* Her mind was starting to put the pieces together.

If it was passed down to him, it was for one reason, and one reason alone. She gasped, the idea clarifying itself, though it still felt out of reach. Incomprehensible. If that man was killed by such a thing, and my father died the same night, then that means my father was a Siapheg and killed the Captain, and then he was killed by the Teselym for doing such a thing… or my father was the Teselym, and the Siapheg killed the man, and then killed my father, possibly. But why?

Her father had never hurt a fly, not in all the years she had known him, so why would he kill someone the night he died? She stuffed the Dracosinum under the cushion beneath her head and closed her eyes. I'm going mad to think that all of this mythology is real. There is nothing to balance good and evil, but the gods themselves. If anyone knew what I am considering this night, I would be committed for sure. Just as the sun started to rise, she finally fell asleep.

When Wylie awoke, she was in a strange bed, and the smell of coffee invaded her nostrils. Coffee, a luxury she was never able to afford. Looking around, she saw a small three-legged stool next to the bed with a glass of water on it. Realizing she was no longer on the bench she had fallen asleep on, the Dracosinum immediately came to mind, and she searched the bedding thoroughly for it. Not finding it, she jumped up and rushed out into the shop.

"Where's the Dracosinum?" She demanded, not giving a thought to the two men and a woman who were there browsing. Her appearance surprised them, and one of the men snickered softly.

Dr. Mullins grabbed her roughly by the elbow and guided her into the back room, from where she had come.

"Shh... Do you want the whole world to know?" Her eyes widened at his sudden gruffness, and his firm grip on her arm. "Did you even look, or like a chav of a girl, did you just assume I had stolen it?" A blush of embarrassment crept into her cheeks.

"My apologies, Dr. Mullins. It was a shock to find it missing."

"Well, for a woman who requires a certain level of discretion, you certainly didn't think about the fact that I might have customers? Or that your tousled hair and wrinkled clothes may cause said customers to think some funny business took place here last night? I have a professional image to uphold, miss."

"You have a professional image to uphold? What of my virtue?"

"You are the one who came into the shop with all guns blazing."

She huffed, "How dare you! What have you done with my Dracosinum? As soon as it's in my hands, I will be well on my way."

He walked over to a shelf that contained a number of books, and grabbed the Dracosinum, thrusting it into her hands.

"Here," he turned his back and walked away from her. Wylie would have run straight out, at that very moment, except her gallies were missing from her feet. She glanced around for them, but they didn't appear to be in the room. She decided they must be out in the shop area but wisely chose to wait for the customers to leave before running out willy-nilly again.

The memories of the previous night played themselves out in her mind. She turned the Dracosinum over and over in her hand, admiring the emeralds. She wished she could sell it for what it was worth, but knew that the information she had learned last night would ensure that would never happen. If she was to accept the contents of the book as fact, it was more than likely that keeping the Dracosinum in her possession was key to her future. She would have to find another way to save Lugwallow Parish.

Lugwallow. The widow Turpin! What would the widow Turpin think of my overnight absence? She heard exchanges of pleasantries in the shop, and the door open and close, so she knew it was safe to go out and look for her boots. There they stood as plain as day near the front door as if waiting patiently for her to retrieve them. Slipping them on and lacing them up, she felt Dr. Mullins eyes on her.

"My apologies for earlier, Dr. Mullins. You have been nothing but a gentleman to me. Please, how much do I owe you for allowing me to sleep here last night?"

He waved his hand as if to stop her. "Nonsense, I don't want your money. I am the one who should be apologizing. I've just been a bit riled up. I was a boy when I first heard of the Dragaleth, but at that age, it was just a game to me. A fun story. Never in a million years would I have thought it to be true. Except, the item you have in your possession is so exquisite that I imagine that a god must have created it. Also, I have to apologize because I said I wouldn't disturb you while you were sleeping, but this morning when I went to wake you, you were sleeping so soundly, I simply picked you up and carried you to my bed before I opened the shop."

"I didn't realize you had tucked the Dracosinum under your pillow. It hit the floor pretty hard, but when I went back to examine it, I saw there wasn't a single scratch on it. I suspect it has some sort of protection or spell on it to keep it safe," he said as he continued his work, his voice softer than it had been earlier.

"Yes, I found that to be true myself. I've dropped it a time or two as well. Anyway, I must be on my way. My home parish is in trouble, and I'm sure my absence will raise questions." She nodded politely at him, tucking the Dracosinum in her pouch once more.

"Yes, yes, I understand. Just a moment, please." He raised one finger as he walked back to his dusty workspace and picked up the ragged leather book with its buckles and straps that informed Wylie of her destiny. "Here, it's likely you will need this more than I. Take it. Please." His gaze was earnest.

"Oh, I can't! I can't do that, Doctor."

"If you are sent here by the gods as that book indicates, then I've fulfilled my purpose by giving that book to the person who truly needs it. Maybe you can put in a good word for me?" he said as he smiled.

Wiley simply grinned in return, completely overwhelmed by the doctor's kindness.

"If it is as this book says, I'll make sure you get a special reward, Dr. Mullins," she replied, her eyes tearing up at his unexpected generosity. Her stomach growled, reminding her that she had been away from home too long and also reminding her of her other duties, to feed Lord Adrian's horses. "Thank you for your kindness! Truly, thank you!" He nodded, giving her another stubble-faced grin as she hurried out into the day. Her eyes were immediately assaulted by the bright sunshine.

"Don't forget to stop by if you ever need anything!" he called after her. Wylie nodded agreement as the shop door closed behind her.

It felt like she had been hidden away in a cave for years, and it took her a moment to acclimate. Had she been so caught up in her own petty drama that a whole day had passed? Had she really stayed the night with a strange man, in his shop? God help me if anyone I know gets wind that I stayed the night with an older man, alone. I'll never hear the end of it.

She tucked the worn book under her arm and set off at a brisk pace. She tried to straighten her hair out as she went, re-braiding it tighter, and checked that her goggles were securely in place. She was not used to getting to Lord Adrian's stables so late. Surely, he would chastise her for doing so, and the fear in her heart made her hurry all the more. Now that Adrian's father had passed, and he had professed his true feelings, Wylie was sure he would take whatever actions necessary to cover up those feelings for her. She was almost certain that would involve firing her.

Never in a million years would he allow anyone to think less of him, nor would she want them to. If anyone found out the truth, it may quite possibly destroy everything that Lord Adrian's family had worked to build. She smiled to herself once again daydreaming about his handsome face. She would adore being Lady Wylie McCollum. She imagined servants laying out her fine dresses day after day. Having her clothes scented of lilac and smelling like a small slice of heaven. She allowed the warm thoughts and daydreams of a fairytale lifestyle to carry her swiftly to the stables.

The sun was once more beginning to set just as Wylie was arriving. She wasted no time, dragging sacks of grain to their feeding troughs. A servant had set out a fresh crate of apples and carrots, and she grabbed several of each, mixing them with their grain so that they could snort through and find the treats. The moment Chaos caught wind of her scent, he nickered loudly.

"Hello Chaos, my lovely." She ran her hand over his soft nose as she walked past. Like brushing velvet, she had lost count of the number of times she had laid her head against it and shared her sorrows. After she had fed them all, she slipped a halter on Chaos and led him out of his stall to brush him. "Chaos, I don't know how much longer I can be here."

He nickered and stamped his left leg.

"I know, I love you, too." She let out a long exasperated sigh. "Soon you will have a new mistress." A tear rolled down her face. Losing her father, her home, and now possibly her job. It was all a bit much. She groomed his luxurious black coat with great care as she told him about the Dragaleth and what she had learned. She was trying hard to wrap her mind around all that had happened in the last day and a half. When she was finished brushing him, she led him back to his stall and rested her head against his neck, his coarse mane tickling her nose.

The day was rapidly turning to night. She had been nearly twenty-four hours without food, and though the hunger pains had come and gone, she knew she needed to get home. It wasn't such a long walk, but the looming darkness felt threatening, even with a gun tucked in her belt. She wasn't sure how safe she felt. She closed Chaos back in his stall and patted the mares before taking a deep breath of resolve and heading off to Lugwallow. She kept her hand on the butt of the little gun, holding it firmly as she walked, afraid a robber or some other undesirable would try to come after her.

Having worked herself into quite a tizzy, she soon realized it was too cold for most people to be on the street, and the beggars she passed were more interested in seeking warmth. The one moment when she thought she heard something, she pulled her gun so fast and turned around to face whoever was following her that the beggar took one look at her and ran off into a dank and dirty alleyway. The look on his face was one of pure fear.

"Edward! Oh, I'm terribly sorry! I didn't mean to frighten you." She immediately felt guilt at her actions. She hadn't meant to scare poor old Mr. Palmer. He was as harmless as they came, and she often brought him fruit or bread on her way home from Lord Adrian's. He had already retreated to the alleyway and showed no sign of coming back out, which only deepened her guilt. I'll make sure to pick him up something extra special to eat tomorrow, to make up for it, she resolved.

Getting back to her home couldn't happen soon enough for Wylie. One day felt like an eternity being away from the only place she really felt safe. Even the rough time the door gave her when she had to yank it open didn't bother her. She happily locked it behind her, sliding the latches into place. She needed a warm bath and a long sleep, but most importantly, food.

She set about lighting the stove, anxious to use as little gas as possible, but needing to cook a few vegetables as well as heat water for her bath. She would have to pump the water and then heat it on the stove, but it was so much better than trying to bathe with cold water. She would bathe and then eat, and in the morning she would visit the widow Turpin to find out what the people of Lugwallow Parish had decided to do.

CHAPTER TEN

The golden sunlight streaming in the next morning comforted Wylie with its welcome warmth. She had fallen asleep in her father's bed again, and the familiar scent of him invading her nostrils caused her emotions to waver between nostalgic pleasure and pain from his loss.

As she sat up, the weight of something heavy in her hand drew her attention.

"The Dracosinum." She didn't even remember pulling it from its protective pouch on her utility belt. How did this get around my neck? She remembered going to bed in a nightgown, but she also remembered placing her utility belt on the dresser. What on God's

Earth is happening? She stared severely at the Dracosinum, willing it to tell her its secrets, but it remained uncooperative. "Do you have something to do with my foggy memory?"

Just then, loud knocking came from the front door, startling her so that she nearly dropped the thing on the ground. Lord Adrian, again? Had he come to see her for the second day in a row? Her heart nearly burst from the anticipation of seeing his face. Perhaps he had decided against marrying Judith. Perhaps the agony of his love was too much, and he realized that he must marry Wylie and steal her away to Dobbinsturn, to be Lady of his estate.

"Fairy tales, Wylie. Pull yourself together... you're far too level-headed for this sort of nonsense." Or so she had thought, but then again, that was before the idea of the dragon myth had invaded her imagination. She leaned out of her father's room and yelled, "I'll be there as soon as I can." Lord Adrian would not catch her off-guard today. She would wear her corset and brush her hair before answering the door. When she was properly dressed, and feeling somewhat like a lady, she rushed to the door and opened it with a radiant smile on her face. "Please your Lord..." But it was not Lord Adrian that greeted her.

"Lady Judith. What are you doing here?" she asked, her smile fading.

Judith couldn't meet her eyes, and simply mumbled,

"My father has sent me to inform you that you have ten days to vacate your residence before he comes and evicts you himself." Lady Judith put a small leather pouch which clinked with coins in Wylie's palm, along with an official looking paper with the large word EVICTION printed at the top. "It's not a lot, but it will help you find another place. I am so very sorry, Wylie. I tried to stop him."

"Like Hell you did!" Wylie shouted, tossing the purse back at her. "I don't want your money, it's traitor's money, and I will have none of it!" Judith stepped back in alarm at Wylie's outburst as two men stepped down from the carriage, straightening their suits as they came to Lady Judith's side.

"Wylie, your stubbornness would see you on the streets in your corset and bloomers! Where will you go without any coin?" Lady Judith thrust the pouch back at her. "Please, please take it. You are still my friend, and I still love you. This is my father's doing, not mine. No matter what happens between us, I would never want you on the street." Wylie huffed, slamming the door in Judith's face, her heart racing.

How dare she come to my home! With her father's men, as if she needs protecting!? I'll die before I take their money!

"Wylie? Please, Wylie… after all of our years of friendship… is this how it will be?"

Wylie could not bring herself to answer. If Lady Judith was any sort of a friend, she would not be at her door trying to evict her from her home at the order of her father. Wylie, if you were her friend, you would not be in love with her fiancé, her subconscious shot back. She knew that was true and realized at that moment; she would not fight Lord Jameston. She would take her tiny bit of savings and leave Lugwallow Parish for good. Maybe take a ship to northern England and search for work there. She knew how to do a great many things; she might work as a shop hand, a stable girl, a cook, a maid… there were any number of things she was capable of. Perhaps a well-off family would hire her as a nanny, and she could spend her days caring for children.

The idea sounded wonderful; it would certainly be a change from what she had always known.

"Wylie, please?" Lady Judith had still not left, and so she opened the door once more.

"My mind is made up, I will not take money from a traitor. As for you and I, we are no longer friends, so you don't have to feel guilty about casting me out into the streets." Wylie spoke with steely resolve, but inside, her heart was breaking. They had been friends for as long as she could remember. Her fondest memories were horseback riding, picnics, and airship-watching with Judith. There had been a time when she had dreamed of being the captain of the most glorious airship in the sky, and Lady Judith had fully supported her. Tears welled up in her eyes and saw that Lady Judith's eyes had gone red with tears as well. They turned away from each other as Lady Judith made her way back to the carriage where one of the men assisted her up the step.

There was no more to be said. Wylie shut the door on Judith for the last time and listened with a sinking heart as the horses clopped away. By the sound, she knew they had only gone a few feet, and she heard the heavy thudding as they knocked on the door to inform the widow Turpin of her eviction. Wylie walked back to her father's room and sat on his bed, fresh tears falling fast and free down her cheeks.

"There is nothing left for you here, Wylie girl. Time to get a move on." She knew it was true, but the sudden memory of the Dracosinum flashed in her mind. What had it said about the next Dragaleth accepting their destiny? She wiped her face on her sleeve and snatched up the journal that Dr. Mullins had given her the day before. She flipped it open, scrolling through the aged pages to what she was looking for.

The human host is only able to summon the Dragaleth when they are of an age to understand the balance between good and evil. This will be evidenced when they hold the Dracosinum in one hand, and the dragon essence balances perfectly. The gear will line up in accordance with its internal workings, but only on nights when the moon aligns with the North Star.

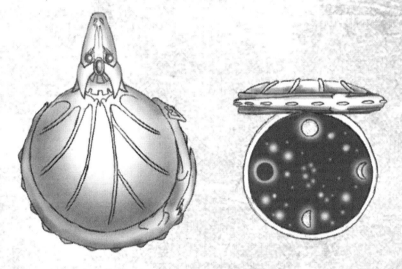

To activate the dragon essence within, the human host must turn the crown of the Dracosinum a total of twelve full turns to the left, and five full turns to the right. This act will unlock the essence of the dragon within and complete the connection with the human host. Once activated, it cannot be undone, and if the human host finds or inherits a Dracosinum and decides not to activate it, the Earth and its people will be left to destroy themselves as the balance of good and evil will eventually run out.

Though I have referred to the possessor of the Dragaleth as a host, make no mistake that the Dragaleth and the human who possesses it, are one and the same, for it is the essence of the person them self and it has been discovered that one cannot exist without the other. This concludes my findings.

Thaddeus McCollum

Wylie spoke to herself out loud to commit what she'd just read to memory. "So, I must hold the Dracosinum and wait to see if the dragon essence balances. If that works, then I must turn the crown of the Dracosinum a total of twelve turns left, and five turns right. Then it will be revealed whether or not I am aware? I wonder what it means by the Earth and its people will be left to destroy themselves as the balance of good and evil will eventually run out."

"What if I am the Siapheg? What if I am the evil dragon and I do something horrible?" Wylie couldn't imagine how she would feel if she knew for sure that she was the Siapheg. She didn't want to be the one responsible for the death and destruction of her friends and loved ones. It was too much to bear, even to think about. She held the Dracosinum in her hand and stared at it, wondering how different it would be now that she knew its truth. Would it do something different? Will I do something different? Lost in thought, her eyes eventually settled on the name Thaddeus McCollum.

It was as if she was seeing it for the first time.

"McCollum! Like Lord Adrian McCollum? That can't be possible!" She flipped the pages once more, looking for dates. The timeline that Thaddeus had constructed covered the late 1200s to the mid-1300s. There were no dates for when he had recorded his findings though she imagined they couldn't be far off from what he had written on the timeline. Surely there was no link? It had to be a coincidence?

The idea set her mind reeling, and rather than sit and stare at the Dracosinum, she decided she would pay a visit to Lord Adrian's stables. He wouldn't know anything about her findings, and it was unlikely she would have the chance to discuss it with him anyway. She needed to get away from her thoughts and the negativity of the morning's activities. There was nothing else to be done this very moment, anyway.

Lord Jameston had more money than she could ever hope to have unless she was willing to sell the Dracosinum, but now that she knew of its importance, there was no possibility of that happening either. She needed to go somewhere familiar to work and think, and the stables were the perfect place for that. She slipped out of her gown and corset and pulled on trousers, work chemise, and vest. Finally, she slid on her mucked up gallies and grabbed her goggles. She needed to be out of the house as quickly as possible.

As she took to the street, locking the door behind her, she could see the elegant satin back of the carriage that was bearing Lady Judith from house to house. Wylie imagined that there was much sadness and mourning in Lugwallow as the people she cared about found out one by one that they had a short ten days to pack their belongings and find a suitable place to live. The thought made her stomach turn; the fact that what Lord Jameston was doing was completely legal, or at least appeared that way, was sickening.

Wylie's anger made her want to kick the carriage wheel so maliciously it would break so that Lady Judith and her fancy assistants would have to walk back to Dobbinsturn. She imagined the mud splattering their layers of velvet and silks. That was something that would infuriate Lady Judith no end. Instead, Wylie took a different route to avoid the carriage altogether and hurried off to Lord Adrian's estate.

It had been three days since Lord Adrian's unprecedented and entirely inappropriate visit to her home. She wondered if he had thought about her as much as she had thought of him and decided probably not. She chided herself for her selfish thoughts, for surely, he had been arranging a funeral over the course of the past few days. Most likely, he would have his father buried by week's end. She wanted to knock on the door of his home and offer him solace. For who better to comfort him than she, who had lost her own father just a fortnight and three days before.

"Good day, Chaos. Good day, ladies," Wylie called out in greeting as she entered the stable. The horses flared their nostrils and stomped their hooves in response. She doled out their allotment of oats, then talked cheerfully to them as she shoveled out their stalls and did their daily grooming. She was still expecting a visit from a servant or someone of importance to tell her she no longer had a job. If not that very day, she was sure it would happen the moment Lady Judith told Lord Adrian about Wylie's behavior.

"You... You're here?" Lord Adrian's voice stammered from where he stood by the stable door.

"Lord Adrian," she exclaimed in surprise.

"Wylie..." his voice a mixture of relief and concern, "You're okay?"

She laughed at his odd response. "Of course, I'm okay! Why wouldn't I be?"

"I just got word there was another beast attack," he responded.

"What? Surely not here?"

"No, Wyles. In Lugwallow... I was so afraid it was you." He rushed to her, placing his hands on her shoulders. Her breath quickened the moment he touched her.

"Lugwallow? Surely you must be mistaken. I would have heard if such a thing happened. I've just come from there." She tried to think back over her route out of town. She had gone a different way to avoid passing Lady Judith's carriage. "That's so strange! I wonder who was killed."

"I don't know, I'm just so relieved it wasn't you." Without asking as he had done before, he gathered her in his arms and pulled her close. "I don't know what I would do if I lost both you and my father." He laid his chin atop her head, gathering her hands in his.

"Dearest Lord Adrian, I don't know how much longer I can go on this way. This incessant game of wondering and worrying."

"Wondering and worrying about what?" he inquired, stepping back, but still holding her hands firmly.

"Aren't you worried we will be caught? What if Lady Judith finds out? She will make you get rid of me, and then I will be out of employment as well as a home." Wylie's head dropped, and she stared at the hay-strewn floor of the stable.

"Nonsense! You will never lose employment with me! What would give you that idea?"

"You said yourself, she knows! After this morning's exchange with her, I imagine she will want me out of here as quickly as possible."

He let go of one hand and lifted her chin to meet his gaze.

"She knows I don't love her, I have yet to tell her who I truly love, but it matters not. Our wedding is in a month's time, and I must do the honorable thing. Until then, I consider myself a free man, and I wish to spend whatever free time I can with you." He bent his head, touching his lips to hers, and sent her heart careening out of control.

When he pulled away, she was breathless.

"It's not right… what we are doing is not right…" Wylie contested.

"I know, it breaks every rule. My father would be disgusted, but I don't care. He never knew love with my mother, only convenience. He told me so himself. Probably the downside to having money, I imagine. It's not often we get to marry for love. Though, I do believe my betrothal is the earliest one I have heard of in this sordid family." He leaned forward, pulled her closer to him, and kissed her again.

"My Lord…" she muttered.

He held her tighter, "You do not always have to have something to say, my love."

She grinned impishly.

"No, I suppose you get enough of that from Judith."

"That I do," he agreed.

She carefully wrapped her arms around his neck, afraid the very act would get them seen by unwanted eyes. Everything in her that was reasonable and intelligent vanished the moment he kissed her. She wanted desperately to warn him, to tell him to save himself, but instead she asked, "How are things going with the funeral arrangements?" She realized the question might make him sad, but she wanted him to know she was concerned.

"As well as to be anticipated I suppose, his death was sudden. Another downside to money is that people look distastefully upon you if you exhibit emotions that are not favorable," he confessed.

"Do you mean to tell me you are not permitted to grieve?" She thought back on the nights she had mourned her father's death; even now, she felt like crying just at the mention of his name. "To mourn is human…" she whispered softly.

"Yes, well... tell that to the executors of my father's estate, the servants, the maids, and all the people that have come in and out of the house in the past few days. Their faces so stern, I assume they're stuck that way. The moment I began to get a bit emotional, you would have thought a plague had struck the room. They rushed out of there without so much as a word of acknowledgment of my grief. He was my father, for better or for worse. He gave me the life I have and made me the man I am today."

"Yes, yes… and you should be allowed to grieve without fear of repercussion or without fear of chasing everyone away. It's wretched really, please don't feel like you have to put on a brave face for me. I of all people understand." She brushed a stray curl of dark hair from his forehead.

"I should say the same of you." He leaned forward and kissed her forehead, allowing his lips to linger there for a moment before pulling back.

"I assure you that I am not putting on a brave face, I often feel that coming here to be with Chaos and the girls help me to think. I think much better when my mind is distracted."

He moved his hands lower down to her waist, "Distracted, how?" He offered her a sly grin.

"Well, that's a very good start, except for the life of me, I can't remember what I was going to say," she said as a crimson blush stained her cheeks.

"Well, tell me of this exchange between you and my betrothed today? What of that? What did you mean you would be out of employment and a home? You can rest assured nothing she says has any weight around here." He winked as if to reassure her, but the act just made her gloomier.

"Adrian, please do not think poorly of Judith for what I am about to tell you. I do not wish to cause dissension between you and her," she said as her forehead furrowed in worry.

"You must not fret, my love. What occurred just now between us is all my doing. I would not let you take the blame for that. Now, tell me what happened?" he insisted.

Wylie took a deep breath, realizing if she told him he would think poorly of Lady Judith and may very well call off the wedding.

"Oh, Adrian. I am a horrible person for what I am about to say." She sucked in a deep breath and continued, "just a few short days ago, the day Judith wished to speak to me alone here, and she sent you away, she warned me that her father was going to partner with investors to purchase all of Lugwallow. At first, I thought it a splendid idea; new investors would have the money to clean it up and help the poor who live there.

"But that was never their intention. She informed me that her father and the investors mean to purchase Lugwallow and kick all those who live there, out onto the street, so they can tear down the houses and build new ones."

"Surely her father is not that heartless?" Adrian was obviously taken aback.

"That's what I thought. I thought for certain no one could do that to innocent men, women, and children. Then today, as I awoke, someone was pounding on my door. I thought it was you but when I answered, it was Lady Judith presenting me with an eviction notice and trying to place a purse of money in my hands. She informed me I need to leave my home within ten days or I will be jailed." Adrian dropped her hands, and took several steps back, his face turning purple with rage.

"That is the most detestable thing I've ever heard!" he yelled, his voice startling Wylie and the horses. The mares stomped back and forth loudly in their stalls in alarm, and Chaos let out a loud neigh, tossing his head up and down. Wylie immediately rushed to his side, patting his coarse mane, and whispering, "It's okay, boy…" Over and over.

"I can't believe that Lord Jameston would do such a thing! I'll put a stop to it! Rest assured! This will not take place while I am around to prevent it."

"No, please! Adrian! You mustn't say anything! You will ruin your reputation. You will lose everything! You mustn't say a word. Please! I never wanted to anger you…"

"But if I know what is right and do nothing, just to save face, doesn't that make the evil of the situation all the greater?"

"Adrian, you would not have known about it, but for me. Please... I beg of you, don't say anything. You have already given me so much... more than I dared hope for. I don't wish you to jeopardize your social status on my account." Tears streamed down her face as she patted the soft velvet of Chaos's muzzle.

"I have been nothing but selfish with my feelings and actions. I have done as I damn well pleased, knowing that I could not marry you, but still accepting your love for my own. I will only break your heart in the end, Wylie. You must allow me this one thing. It's the least I can do."

It was Wylie's turn to walk toward an angry-faced Adrian. She cupped his lovely, aristocratic face in her work-roughened hands and stared deeply into his gray eyes.

"No, Adrian. You mustn't. Please. My love is mine to give to whom I please, and because I chose to reciprocate your feelings does not mean you took advantage or that you are selfish. I gave my heart to you, and in return, you gave me moments of joy. Several beautiful moments in which my station in life didn't matter, in which I felt loved and beautiful... there is nothing more wonderful than that. If I never fall in love again, it will be enough. I want you to marry Judith and be happy with her. Be the great Lord Adrian McCollum of Dobbinsturn that you are meant to be."

"How could I profess to love you if I allowed you to be thrown out on the streets?" His gray eyes had darkened like the fury of a hundred storm clouds threatening to destroy a town.

"Love me enough that you promise not to compromise yourself for my sake."

"Haven't I already done that by being seen in Lugwallow? By kissing you here, on the very property where my betrothed will live in just a short month? What is one more act of defiance?"

"Then promise me that you will not compromise yourself again, in any way," she pleaded.

"Do you mean to say that I may not kiss you either?"

She nodded, "Our lips must never again meet. I would be unable to live with myself if I cost you your home or your station in life."

"Wylie, why are you asking this of me?" His voice had grown hoarse with emotion.

"Adrian... Lord Adrian... The moment you hired me into your employ, I knew that I loved you. How could I not? You have demonstrated nothing but kindness to me at every turn, but I never thought in a lifetime... in a million lifetimes that I would receive that love in return. Now, I want you to be everything your father wanted you to be because that is what love is. You will be a great

141

man, and if she ever leaves you, I will be here. You need only say the word, and I will be at your side."

"I have a responsibility to her, but my heart is yours," he argued.

"And I will never take advantage of that, m'Lord." She bowed gracefully. "Now, please… please let me finish my work here and return home before I lose my self-control and do something that both of us will regret." If he didn't leave straight away, she knew she would kiss him again, and then she would never leave his side, even if he begged.

Adrian straightened his waistcoat and top hat and looked for a moment as if he were going to grab her again. She shook her head 'no' tears still falling, so he walked slowly but purposefully out of the stable, back towards the house. She watched him intensely until he had disappeared from sight, then let out a huge sigh. She couldn't continue to work today; it was all too much.

She gave the horses their hay and then took off running towards home. Her heart felt as if it had been ripped from her chest. The only love she had ever known was someone she had no business loving. Maybe she really was a Siapheg.

No matter, she knew what she must do. She must turn the crown of the Dracosinum as per the instructions and accept her fate. Even if it was for the worse.

CHAPTER ELEVEN

The moment Wylie arrived in Lugwallow, she knocked on the widow Turpin's door.

"Mrs. Turpin, please... are you home?" She knocked again, and again.

"Yes, yes, Wylie, what is it?"

"Have you spoken to the people of Lugwallow? Are they willing to fight? Have they come up with a plan?"

"Why yes, my dear. We have. We have decided it is time for us to move on from this place. A lot of us have lost loved ones here, and a new start doesn't seem like such a bad idea. Lord Jameston was quite generous in his dealings today. I am not the only one who thinks so, either. The money he gave us is more than enough to set up somewhere else, and we're okay with that."

"You can't be serious, Mrs. Turpin? What about the history here? What about the good memories? Are you going to throw that all away because a rich man has given you enough to start over somewhere else? I don't understand why he didn't just take that money that he gave all of us and invest it back into Lugwallow? It would be more than enough to clean up the streets, homes, and shops."

"Yes, my dear, it makes no sense to me either. Unfortunately, I am too old to fight the man, and sitting in a jail cell penniless, then homeless when I'm let out, doesn't sound like a good plan either. I and the others are going to take advantage of the opportunity and maybe you should too." The widow softly closed the door in Wylie's face, but Wylie stuck her foot between the door and the frame to stop it.

"One further thing, Mrs. Turpin, did you hear of a death that took place here last night? Do you know who it was?"

"Yes, it was that homeless fellow. What's his name? Edward Palmer. You knew him, didn't you? I saw you give him a bit of bread a time or two. He was attacked by an animal of some sort. The constable is convinced it was a wild dog." Wylie's foot slipped out of the door; it was too much to bear.

Wylie ran out into the middle of the street, threw her head back, and let out the loudest, most forceful yell she could manage. It garnered her a few open doorways and peeps from behind curtains, but no one bothered to ask her what was the matter. Poor Mr. Palmer dead. He'd never hurt a fly.

She had only recently found out about the Dracosinum, and now someone in her town ends up dead? It couldn't have been a coincidence.

It was as she feared... she must be the Siapheg. Even if she didn't completely accept it, it was her purpose. The only thing she could do was give in to it. Gradually Wylie returned to her senses, realizing she was still standing in the middle of the street. With an effort, she pulled herself together and withdrew into her house. This time with stronger convictions than she had mustered in a great while. She wasn't totally clear how the transformation worked, but she seized the Dracosinum from its pouch and went into her father's room, confident that if there were a place it would work best, it would be there.

The room where her predecessor had once slept. Never in a million years could she have dreamed the peculiar direction her life would take, or that she would live out a mythology in her lifetime. It was all so surreal. She sucked in a deep breath, and holding the Dracosinum in her hand, she opened the winged cover, watching for any change in its appearance.

Then, an extraordinary thing happened as she did so. The mechanical apparatus that had previously only risen up and outward, took on a mind of its own and lifted directly over and above the dragon pictured on the face of the device. When the holes lined up exactly with the ones around the dragon's body, it stopped and rested there patiently, almost as if waiting for her to make another move.

"Well, it's now or never." Wylie turned the crown of the Dracosinum twelve full turns to the left, noting for the first time the slight little notch in the knob which lined up with the full moon inside the Dracosinum 's face. Then she turned it a full five turns to the right. As she did so, a soft clicking and whirring sound began to come from the instrument, and the dragon inside the device appeared to come alive.

She watched in utter fascination as the dragon glided around inside the Dracosinum, completely at home in its tiny enclosure, before coming to rest on the first star, located precisely where the first hour would be indicated in an ordinary pocket watch. The little fellow stared up at her earnestly as if something remained for her to do, but for the moment she hadn't the foggiest notion what that was.

She had accepted her fate. If she was the Siapheg, let the chips fall where they may. Should she sit? Should she pace? What was she waiting for?

"What am I waiting for Dracosinum?" she inquired of the tiny dragon on the face of the irritating apparatus. It blinked up at her in expectation. She must have given herself into lunacy to believe she was seeing what her eyes told her she was seeing. The tiny creature's wings gave an agitated little shake. Overwhelmed, and annoyed from the events of the day, she felt herself growing sleepy.

"I give up!" she said forcefully, falling back onto the bed before closing her eyes and drifting off. The moment her eyes closed, something else inside her awakened. In her mind it was as if she was dreaming; while her body remained on the bed, she felt herself rise up from it and walk around in a sort of half sleep. She waved her hands in front of her, but she couldn't see clearly enough to determine what the little flickers of blue were in front of her eyes.

Am I a ghost? Why can't I see clearly? She felt so utterly weightless, it was if she could float away.

The feeling was so déjà vu, and yet she knew at that moment that she had felt this several times before, and now she was doing it again with full knowledge of what was to come. She didn't waste a single moment; her body braced itself for what it already knew and had simply waited for her mind to discover.

A tingling began at the base of her spine and traveled upward until she was suffused with a glorious tingling sensation. It was positively delightful, the feeling of accepting her new self. From her face grew an iridescent white snout, and from behind, she grew a long splendidly luminescent tail. The point of the tail was as well-defined as a recently sharpened blade.

It flicked of its own accord, with her joy of discovery.

I am not the Siapheg! The realization was like a drink of the finest wine, and she blinked away a tear, so overtly thankful that she did not possess such evil inside of her. The only problem, she now realized, was that she must now discover who the dark one is so she can put a halt to the suffering it may bring. The tingling eased off, and she sat on the edge of her father's bed completely transformed.

"Why, I'm no larger than a house cat. How strange."

"Not so strange, young Teselym."

"Huh?" Wylie jumped up, alarmed by the sound of another's voice. She promptly lost her balance and tumbled off the bed. She hit the floor with a solid thunk.

"Don't worry Teselym; your body is capable of many beautiful and magnificent things. Your size will adapt to your circumstances once you leave this room. You can also make yourself smaller if you wish. Anything you desire, you need only state it. The magic that lies within you will do the rest. Consider it compensation from the gods."

Her white scaled head turned this way and that as she searched for the owner of the voice, but there was no one to be seen. "Who is that?"

"Must I answer that if you can't even find me?"

Wylie huffed in response, "I need to be larger." Instantly she began to grow, and shortly she was roughly the size of a large dog. The mattress was now at eye level, and she looked around for the Dracosinum, wondering where it had gone.

"You may call it you know."

"Call what?" Wylie asked, agitated that she had not found the source of the voice.

"The Dracosinum, it is yours… all you have to do is call it, and it will come to you. Do you think you found its hiding place by yourself? Not hardly, m'dear."

"Dracosinum, come to me," Wylie commanded firmly. The circular device lifted itself from her human form which lay still on the bed and hovered in midair before her. Wylie reached for it, agitated that it was so much harder to grab with dragon claws than human fingers. The seemingly simple action now required much more effort.

The moment she held it, the blasted thing opened of its own accord and the clear crystal that protected the tiny beast inside flipped open, revealing its tiny tenant sitting happily in the center with an impudent grin on his face.

"There, now… was that so hard?" The tiny dragon spoke.

She almost dropped the Dracosinum, but quickly gathered her senses. "Oops, sorry about that?" she said by way of apology.

"Another little trick, so you don't have to go through that again. Every time you become the Teselym, your Dracosinum will be attached to you. Without it, you don't have me, and without me you are vulnerable and naïve."

"I beg your pardon? Just who are you?" She lifted the Dracosinum closer to her face, to see the vexatious little bugger better.

"Well, it's all a bit tricky to understand. I mean, I don't presume the human part of you would be able to comprehend," he said matter-of-factly.

"Why you insolent, insulting little beastie!"

"I guarantee you, my dear Wylie, that is not my intention at all. To answer your question and quell any further questions you may have, I am a god, or at least the essence of a god. My sole purpose is to help you reach your full potential as the Earth's one and only Teselym. You are the only thing standing between mankind and complete and utter evil." He nodded his head knowingly, sitting back on his haunches, short scaly arms crossed over his chest like an indignant child.

"Most curious," Wylie said.

"Indeed," he replied.

"The name Dracosinum, what does it stand for?"

"Well, it's Latin… Draco… meaning dragon, of course. Sinum meaning pocket."

Wylie giggled.

"So you're literally a pocket dragon?" The idea hit her in the funny bone, and she guffawed loudly, while he stared back at her unamused.

"Maybe so, but I can be as large as I like." He responded indignantly.

"My apologies. I didn't mean to insult you....?"

She let the question linger in the air, while he sat on the Dracosinum, his arms folded huffily. He didn't pick up on her unasked question.

"Did the gods give you a name with all that spunk, odd little device dweller?"

He gave her a cross look before answering.

"Hmm... nothing permanent. Every Teselym gives me a different name. Though I think this time around, I'd like to be called Quincy. I picked that name up in conversation once, and I happen to like it," he replied.

"So, Quincy it is, may I ask something else? If the gods can send you, why can't they just come down here themselves and handle this business."

"Oh, they can't, they'd break the Earth."

Wylie let out an audible giggle.

"They'd break the Earth? What sort of nonsense is that?"

"You might not believe it, but it's true. If the gods' tears created a race of dragons, what makes you think they wouldn't break the Earth by stepping upon it? Anyway, I'm merely the tiniest piece of them. The smallest piece they could send without causing irreparable damage," he continued, like a wise old owl that had been granted a voice to speak after many years.

"Another question, if I may?"

"Yes, I suppose there will be a great many of those." He seemed slightly agitated. Wylie knew it had to do with her poking fun at him, but she couldn't help it.

"Did you guide my father?"

The little fellow stopped speaking for a moment, all indignation gone from his face, a tear squeezing out of his eye.

"Wylie, your father was one of the most wonderful Teselym I have ever had the privilege of knowing. When he got sick, the Siapheg agreed to leave him be, to let him die in peace. One of the most level-headed Siapheg we have had in all the centuries that I have been here." He dropped to all fours and began pacing back and forth inside the Dracosinum.

"You mean to tell me that you know the Siapheg?" The idea was shocking to her. If this little beast was here to help her balance her moral compass, then what business did he have helping the Siapheg? "You help the Siapheg, as well?"

It was Quincy's turn to laugh, "No, not at all! No way could I help that beast do evil. It wouldn't be right."

"Then does the Siapheg have one such as yourself as well?"

"The Siapheg doesn't need it; it has its own Dracosinum… but there is no reason to balance its moral compass. Its purpose is the direct opposite of yours," he stated matter-of-factly.

"Yes, yes, I figured that out. Shouldn't there be something to govern whether the Siapheg fulfills its evil quota?"

"Unfortunately, since the Siapheg is inherently evil, there is no need to urge it along, it craves evil, death, and destruction intuitively. It does quite well on its own. The whole essence of humanity is inherently evil as a matter of fact. Why do you think there's so much war and death? Do you think the gods encourage that? No, no, no, my dear. For centuries men and women alike have discovered ways to be evil all on their own with no prompting. Almost as if it's easier for them to do what is wrong than to choose what is honorable and right." The poor little fellow looked extremely perplexed at the whole idea.

"Yes, I've noticed that. I'm no better than any of them, giving in to my desires," she sighed deeply. "So, what makes me the least bit qualified for what I must do?"

"Well, besides the fact that it's in your blood... you have me. I do have the power to stop you if you do not fulfill your purpose, and there is always the ability to elect a new Teselym, but breaking the bond is difficult, and time-consuming, so, please... just do what is right? It will be better for the both of us if you do."

Wylie nodded her head at his request. She had nothing on Earth at the moment to keep her from being what she was meant to be. The love in her heart for Lord Adrian was wrong, and acting on it had been even more wrong. She would bottle it up and never think about it again. She simply had to.

"Very well, if you are quite done asking questions, I do believe we get to balancing the good. Do you feel up to it?"

She nodded her head vigorously.

"Though, this isn't my first time, is it?" Wylie asked.

"No, I'm afraid not," he answered.

"Tell me, why don't I remember changing bodies on previous nights?"

"You hadn't chosen it yet. Your body turned instinctively the night your father died. Remember, this is in your blood, your make-up, the very core of who you are. Your soul did what was right until your mind could catch up to the facts, and make a concentrated choice between yes or no. Either accepting it or turning away from it. However, let me say how very glad I am that you chose to embrace it. You are the last of your line, and as I mentioned before, breaking the bond and establishing a new one can be quite difficult."

"So, if I may ask, what happened the moment I found out what the Dracosinum was? I stayed in a gadget shop that night, so I know I didn't transform then."

"That was different, you were suddenly aware of your purpose, whether you had chosen to believe it or not. There are only two ways that being a Teselym works, either you have no conscious thought of the Dragaleths and are ignorant of it, or you know what you must do, and accept it by completing the initiation."

"Initiation?" she inquired.

"The act of turning the winder. It's merely a physical agreement that you have accepted your purpose, but it is required none the less."

"I don't even know what to say."

"No need to say anything, Wylie Petford, we have much to do," There was an urgency in his voice, so she willed herself to become smaller. She shrank to the size of a mouse, so she could crawl through a hole in the wall and make her way outside where she would prepare to take to the skies.

CHAPTER TWELVE

"Magnificent, Wylie. Now, just flap your wings, and they will lift you into the sky where you will adapt to your surroundings." The impish voice came from the Dracosinum which had hung itself around her neck of its own accord the moment she had demanded to be smaller.

The stench of the filthy street invaded Wylie's tiny dragon nostrils with all the fierceness of an invading army.

"Goodness, it is positively rank down here!"

"Well, then I suggest you take to the skies where you belong. Can't very well balance good and evil from the ground."

"No, I don't suppose that I can." Fly to the sky. Her tiny body rose from the ground, her newly acquired, enhanced eyesight able to make out the shape of every creature that moved on the broken streets of Lugwallow, then expanding as she rose higher and higher. Soon she could see Dobbinsturn, then Kinnemore, then all of London was within her sight.

"Too high, let's drift lower. Stay in sight of each city so that you can attend to problems as they arise," came the voice from the Dracosinum.

"Quincy, what exactly do I do now?" The cool night air flowed over her face, and she sucked in a deep breath. There was nothing quite like it. She knew now why airship pilots enjoyed the skies so thoroughly. Now that she had experienced it, she wasn't sure if she ever wanted to leave. Walking about on the streets felt so dreadfully dull by comparison.

"First of all, you must return to Earth daily before the 'Time of Dragons' ends. That's what your Dracosinum is for, it measures your dragon hours. It's a requirement. Secondly, pay close attention to your dragon intuition. It is precise and it will guide you when nothing else does."

"My what?" she asked. Baring her teeth made for a fearsome sight, but Quincy knew it was merely a look of surprise on a very new Dragaleth.

"Your dragon intuition. If you stop talking long enough, you'll pick up on it. It's much like the instinct that tells you right from wrong. Only it will most likely encourage you to fly this way or that; you just need to follow it."

"Well, all right Quincy, if you say so." Teselym Wylie stopped talking for a time and simply drifted happily over the city, and then, like magic, an urging in her mind willed her to fly north as quickly as possible. She followed the feeling, flying past all that was familiar until she came to Leeds. Her mind went so many which ways here; she could barely keep up. She was first led to a dank alleyway which smelled horribly of urine.

A drunken man was forcing a woman against a wall, and though Wylie could smell the scent of other men on her, it was clear this man's drunken advances were not wanted. The woman was crying and pleading with him to leave her alone. Unsure of how to handle the situation, Wylie willed herself invisible, dove down, and grabbed the man by the head as carefully as possible.

His muffled screams from inside her mouth continued while she flew deep into Kinnemore Parish where she dropped him quite abruptly.

He stood up and staggered about, his eyes searching the skies for whatever had picked him up. The sudden flight had sobered him immensely, and he shouted apologies as he ambled around, trying to figure out where he was. Wylie laughed at his stupidity and hurried back to the prostitute she had rescued from him. She could smell her from twenty-five miles away, and as she grew closer, she spied the woman walking back to the brothel she must have called home.

The madam of the house gave her quite the berating when she showed up as Wylie could hear her crying and explaining what had happened. The man who had tried to take advantage of her had robbed her before doing so.

"Never mind getting her money back, you must balance good and evil, not fix every wrong in the world," Quincy admonished, reading her thoughts again.

"How do you do that?"

"I told you, I'm a piece of the gods here to help you and balance you out. How can I do either of those things if I don't know what you are thinking? Now, back to work," he ordered.

Not that his prompting was needed. Already in her mind's eye, Wylie could see a small child crying. She followed the intuitive directions in her head until she found him. At first glance, she thought he was alone, but then the scent of death invaded her nose. She shrank down until she was mouse-sized again and found a way into the house. Pneumonia, the child's mother had died of pneumonia. Though how Wylie knew that was just as much a mystery as everything else she had experienced so far.

"Call it your god-sense."

"What, now?" she asked.

"Special knowledge granted to you that no one else has because you are the Teselym."

"Why do I even bother?" she muttered.

"I know it's all a bit much, Wylie-girl, but you can pretty much be certain that over the next century or so, you'll discover you have a great many amazing capabilities."

"I beg your pardon? Century?" Assuming she had misheard.

"Yes, providing you don't get seriously ill or injured, the Dragaleth have a much longer lifespan than humans do. Your human body will retain its youth much longer as well if that's any consolation."

"I can't process this information right now; I need to help this little boy." With that, she grew larger until she was the size of a large house cat. She appeared before the boy, opalescent as ever, and willed her scales to glow. The little boy backed across the floor to get away from her, evidently afraid of a cat-sized dragon that glowed white.

"Don't worry William; I mean you no harm." She put on her friendliest voice, speaking with the utmost gentleness.

"W—w—what do you want? And how do you know my name?" he stuttered.

"I only want to help you. Will you let me help you?" She came nearer to him, and he reached out his hand to touch her, petting her silky scales with childlike gentleness. He nodded in agreement to her question, and she grew a little bigger. Now the size of a dog, she sat next to him.

"Do you have any other family, child?" He shook his head. The sound of his stomach grumbling reached her ears. "Oh, you poor dear. Let us find something to fill that belly, and then I'll take you somewhere safe, okay?" He nodded his consent.

"Are you an angel?" little William's trembling voice asked.

"My goodness child, far from it. Just someone who wants to help. Come unlatch the door for me, and I'll take you somewhere where you can be fed." He nodded again, and she followed him through the house out of the front door. Once on the street, the boy began to shiver.

"Climb on my back, William." He looked unsure but did so anyway, and when he was safely between her shoulder blades, she willed herself to grow larger and her scales to rise up around him so that he was protected from the elements of the wind and cold as she ascended into the skies.

"What do I do now, Quincy? Do I take him to an orphanage?"

"Good grief, no! Those places are positively dreadful. I happen to know a deserving family, follow my direction."

"Very well Quincy, you know better than I."

He guided her out of London, over the water, to Ireland, to a quaint little cottage that sat alone on an Irish hillside.

"This family has known great sadness over the past few years, having lost all three of their children to one sort of hardship or another," Quincy explained.

"Then how do you know he'll be safe here?"

"The gods have promised them no more loss."

The statement caught her off guard and irritated her at the same time.

"Then why allow for the loss of children at all? Wouldn't it be easier to protect the lives of children than allow them to suffer needlessly?"

"It would seem that way, and though I don't quite understand their reasoning, it does illustrate the point that children, until they reach a certain age, are not evil. Children are naturally good. They do not do things out of hate, spite, or evil nature. At least, the majority of them. To protect them all from the natural disasters that occur, or illness would inherently throw things out of balance."

"That makes no sense!" Wylie contested.

"Yes, well... Take it up with them when you meet them."

"When I meet them?" she exclaimed.

"Yes, after you die, you will meet them. Goodness, did you not know that's what happens?"

Wylie's head was spinning from everything she had been told.

"Let's just take care of this young man and then we can talk more about what is to come," she said. Not wanting to worry the boy, or have him find out too much, she came in close to the cottage Quincy had directed her to and landed gently on the ground, tucking her wings in tight, and scratching at the door with her claws. Then she shrank quickly to the size of a mouse again as they waited for someone to answer.

"Goodness… who could be here at this hour?" came a man's voice from inside.

"I haven't the slightest clue, Daniel. Hurry up… get the door," a woman replied. The man named Daniel opened the door and looked out with a lighted candle.

"Well, what have we here?" The little boy Wylie had rescued stood shivering on the porch. "What's your name, boy?"

"William."

"Well, William… where are your parents?"

"I don't have any. My mother died." He was shaking, and Wylie wished the couple would hurry.

"Are you hungry, boy? Come inside and have something to eat." Daniel put an arm protectively over the boy's shoulders and led him indoors. From her position on the ground, Wylie could see the face of his wife, fresh with tears. She knew instinctively that William was going to be just fine with this couple. The door closed, and the outside went dark once more. Wylie grew larger and rose back up into the sky.

As Wylie spent the night flying nearly worldwide, helping those that she could, she discovered more about herself and her abilities. Her last discovery of the evening was her capability for flash-flying. She needed only to hold the Dracosinum in her talons as she thought of a destination and she was transported there in the wink of an eye.

The wonderment and excitement were overwhelming, and her human emotions barely had time to process the sensations of the night before the sun was rising over London, and she needed to get back home.

Quincy flew ahead of her, enlarging in size so that he could show her some features of the Dracosinum while they flew home,

"When the hand reaches this spot on the Dracosinum, it's time for you to go home, or you will be stuck wherever you happen to be at that moment in your dragon form. Your human body will be like stone at home and unable to be awakened. We have learned from experience that could prove to be disastrous for your human body. To an outsider, it would look like you are dead." It didn't take Wylie long to piece together why that could be a problem.

Wylie stopped flying mid-air, hovering above the city. "Oh dear, I certainly don't want that happening." She held the Dracosinum in her talons and willed herself home, and the next moment, the soft musky scent of her father invaded her nostrils. She was in his room, her body lay exactly where she'd left it on the bed. Seconds later, she felt the tingling run through her body that she had felt when she had changed into the Dragaleth. She experienced the floating sensation again as she glided over to her body, landed on her chest, and the next minute she was sitting upright and breathing, as human as ever. She glanced around the room, aware of how bright everything appeared. Is it morning already?

"Not quite, Princess. We return every morn' just as the sun is peeking over the hills. Just as we have for the past three weeks."

"What?"

"You began transforming the night your father died."

"No! It can't be true!" But just like a floodgate being opened, the moment she said it couldn't be true, she remembered back beyond just the last few nights. It was true and something else she now knew, the blue floating apparition she became as she transitioned from human to dragon was a flame. Not a ghost or an apparition, she had been experiencing the flame every night since her father's death.

"Not a flame exactly, but certainly very like one. That is your soul, your spirit, your essence. It stays the same, your human form is just a shell. Your dragon form is just the potential you have, neither of these things is actually who you are. So the floating flame, as you call it, is your inner being. It's you."

"Why did I not know this?"

"Must I repeat the rule?" he said in exasperation. "You had not yet come into the knowing of your other half,"

"Yes, yes, okay. I get it. It wasn't revealed to me until I knew my purpose, embraced my destiny, that sort of thing."

"Quick one, aren't you?"

"Quincy, I'm mentally exhausted from trying to absorb all this new information. I haven't the energy to spar with you right now. I've got my human day to attend to and you can sit around and be snarky with yourself."

"I shall return to the Dracosinum until you require my assistance once again."

"So, your mouth does stop running at some point? Is that what you're telling me?" she said with a bit of her own snark.

"Of all the female humans in all the land, you're the one I get stuck with?" he retorted.

"I could say the same of you, of all the pieces of the gods, you're the one I get stuck with? Surely they have a superior piece of themselves that would have done me a better service than running its mouth all the time."

"Touché," Quincy replied.

"Now, if you don't mind, I have things to attend to." She slid off the bed and began to prepare for the day ahead.

CHAPTER THIRTEEN

Wylie had awakened feeling more at peace than she had in a long time. Missing her father was something she was gradually learning to deal with. Knowing that he had been a Teselym, working to balance the good side of a precarious world was a consolation to her. Now that it was her purpose as well, it made her feel connected to him somehow. It was almost like he was watching her along with the gods, and one day she would see him, and they would discuss all the marvelous things they had seen.

Wylie felt perfectly able to cope. She would get out of bed and live life just as adequately as before. She still needed to earn a living and eat. Those were factors all human life could be certain of. Today, it was something she was grateful for. Apparently allowing her human body to rest while she flew during her dragon hours, was all the rest she needed.

Life would resume as normal as possible, and Wylie would don her nearly knee-high boots just as she always did, buckling them tightly. She would make her way into Dobbinsturn and take care of Chaos and his stable residents.

Lord Adrian's mournful eyes invaded her mind just then, and the vision almost stole her breath away. One of the drawbacks to being human. Wylie knew she must try very hard not to allow her affections to run away with her again. She would not allow Adrian to fall on her behalf. She prayed that he would stop coming to see her while she worked in the stable. She didn't think she would have the fortitude to turn him away again if he did that. Her eyes grew misty at the prospect of not seeing him or embracing him ever again, but it was only right and proper. As a Teselym it had become even more important that she didn't overstep her limits with him.

The realization that she now had only nine days to figure a way out of her housing situation loomed over Wylie's head as well. If only Judith's father was a reasonable man. If only he could see that he was being merciless, driving many families to move from the very homes that generations of their relatives had grown up in. It made no sense to her. It was heart-wrenching to think that so many of her friends would be moving away shortly.

Get a grip on yourself, Wylie. You have to right this wrong. You will figure it out! She stood tall, after fastening her laces and smoothed her corset down, tucking it into the waistband of her black straight leg trousers, ensuring it fit her delicate frame tightly.

"Yes, I will right this wrong. I have to." She snatched her well-worn, but serviceable, leather utility belt, buckling it at her waist and fastening the smaller strap around her thigh. She slipped the derringer into one of the pockets on the belt, certain she would never leave home again without it. She was grateful for the kindness of strangers and hoped to return the favor to Mr. Webster one day.

The journey to Dobbinsturn passed very quickly as she was preoccupied recalling memories from the night before and wondering about the little boy she had rescued. She sincerely hoped he would form a strong family bond with the couple she had left him with. Lord Adrian's house greeted her with peaceful familiarity, and she found herself excited to see Chaos and his stable mates. Perhaps she would take Lilly out for a ride, she had not taken the mare out in a while, and she doubted Lord Adrian gave her sufficient exercise, as he seemed to favor Chaos.

No matter, I will attend to the others today. Chaos always has my attention. It probably has to do with my love for his master. She sighed heavily, wondering how she'd gotten stuck with the cards she'd been dealt.

When Wylie arrived at the manor, Lady Judith and Lord Jameston were out in the garden talking to Lord Adrian's housekeeper, Miss Davenport. Miss Davenport carried a basket and was cutting flowers for the house. Wylie bypassed them without so much as a glance and hurried to attend to her duties. No matter what situation they were in at the moment, it still saddened her heart to see her former friend.

Wylie desperately needed to stay in focus today and not be distracted by other situations that were lurking. She kept her gaze focused straight ahead as she headed for the stable, wishing she was holding the Dracosinum and could just teleport herself there instantaneously.

"Wylie!" A feminine voice called out behind her. "Please, Wylie. Wait up!"

"Lady Judith!" she spun to face her. "You're looking radiant as usual. How go the wedding plans? Is there anything I can do for you? I am just the stablehand, but I would be more than happy to assist you if needed." Wylie kept her face emotionless, refusing to allow the hurt of her friend's betrayal to show through.

"What? Wylie. I just want to talk to you. I wish to apologize for my father's actions. I don't want it to affect us. You mean a great deal to me, you always have."

"Judith, let's be totally honest here. We can't possibly be the friends I thought we were. For goodness' sake… your father is going to destroy my life and the lives of many others, and let's not forget, I am in love with your fiancé."

Judith looked a bit taken aback,

"Wylie, I don't care that you're in love with him. I certainly am not. Don't you think it bothers me that I will be in a loveless marriage, all for the sake of money? Do you not realize my father forced my hand? Just as much as he is forcing you and yours out of Lugwallow. No one is safe from his greed for riches. Least of all his daughter." The look that came across her lovely face was one of deep sorrow, and Wylie found herself feeling deep empathy toward her friend.

"I guess I owe you an apology, Judith. I've been the most horrible friend… I hope you can forgive me."

"Oh, Wylie! Dang blammit!" Judith cried out, racing toward her and hugging her so tight she felt the breath being squeezed out of her. "We have years of friendship behind us. I wouldn't throw that away for some… cove." She giggled, "Besides, do you not think that I may have found love as well? I've more on my plate than just an unwanted marriage and a tyrant of a father."

"Judith, get over here please. Now!" Lord Jameston barked, so Judith jumped at his command, grabbing Wylie's hand and yanking her along.

"What is 'that' doing here?" he sneered, nodding his head towards Wylie.

"Pardon me, Lord Jameston, with all due respect, which isn't much, I…" Judith clamped her hand over Wylie's mouth and turned to face her father.

"Have we turned into complete monsters, father? Wylie is my friend, and she will always be my friend. And there's nothing you can do about it," she yelled at him. Wylie's eyes grew wide at her friend's outburst.

"You'd better shut your mouth if you know what's good for you, daughter, or your fate will be worse than hers. She has you to thank for what is about to happen next. But first, we have a funeral to attend. There's been another murder."

Judith gasped, "No! Who is it this time?"

"That's not important. Come, we must take our leave." To the housekeeper he said, "Please give Lord Adrian our regards, we shall return in two days to finalize the wedding plans, by which time," and for this, he turned to Wylie, "You'd best be all moved out of your home, or I'll have you jailed!"

"What!?" Wylie and Judith exclaimed at the same time.

"Father! You can't be serious, please don't do this," Judith pleaded, "I am sorry I disrespected you! Please don't punish Wylie."

"I can make it today if you wish?" Lord Jameston continued.

"No. Oh no, Oh Wylie... I'm so sorry!!" Judith wrapped her in a warm embrace, squeezing her with all her might. "I am so, so sorry. I love you like a sister... please forgive my father for this atrocity!"

"I love you, too. Please don't worry about me, Judith. I promise, I'll be okay." Lord Jameston frowned distastefully, and Wylie wished she could take Teselym form and take care of him right then and there.

Lord Jameston called his servant over, and the ladies listened in dismay as he told the dapper man to take word in person to the residents of Lugwallow that they now had two days instead of nine to be packed and moved out or they would be jailed.

Wylie held back tears as he made plans with the servant. Meanwhile, Judith hopped dutifully up into the carriage, tears streaming down her face. They waved to each other until the carriage was out of sight.

The servant took off on horseback, and once both he and Lord Jameston were out of sight, Wylie collapsed on the ground, and let the tears flow. What am I going to do? Where are my people going to go with only two days to pack their things and move?

"If I were a Siapheg, I would rip your throat out!" Wylie screamed out loud, frightening Miss Davenport who was still standing in the garden, a silent witness to her outburst. The woman ran into the house and slammed the door, and Wylie jumped up from the ground and ran to the stables to bury her face in Chaos's mane.

"Hey, hey!" Lord Adrian called after her.

"No, Adrian, don't!" She just couldn't face him. Not now.

"Miss Davenport said you wanted to murder Lord Jameston, what happened?" She spun around and watched his tailcoat flap behind him as he ran after her. His top hat flew off and landed in the dirt. Making no effort to retrieve it, he stopped in front of her, breathless.

"I wasn't serious, not that it's any of your concern." She turned her head away from him, not wanting to meet his eyes or she knew she would buckle.

"You can't do that with me, I see right through you," he said softly. "What happened, love?" Putting an arm around her waist, he pulled her close. She fought to resist, knowing her Teselym side would be having a fit right now if it saw this little exchange.

"Lady Judith and I made up, and as punishment... Lord Jameston says everyone must be out of Lugwallow within two days, or he will have us jailed."

"What? He can't do that!"

"Apparently, you can do a lot of things when you're part of the upper class and have a big purse," she frowned at Adrian. "Like you, with your arm around me right now."

"Huh?" He dropped his hold on her and stepped back. "Whatever do you mean, Wylie?"

"I mean that you're engaged, but because you have money, you think you can just wrap your arms around me, and I'll simply melt," she snapped at him, angry about the situation, and furious at him for being the object of her affections.

"I… I'm not sure why you would say such things, I thought the feelings were mutual?"

Wylie couldn't even bring herself to look into his eyes, instead staring down at his black leather strapped boots.

"Wylie. Please come back to me… you know I don't love Judith. You know that she knows that... The only thing wrong with 'us' is that you are stubborn and refuse to let me give up on responsibilities that I don't even want. You know that she loves someone else? Did you know that? She doesn't want to marry for money either. It's her father. Her father is making her do it."

"She told you she is in love with someone else?" Wylie asked, incredulous.

"Yes, he's a good friend of mine. He isn't too badly off… but he isn't as well to do as I am either. Judith has already spoken to her father about him. He was furious and forbade her to see him ever again," Lord Adrian explained.

"So, you are both sacrificing love for money? Simply because that devil of a man told you to?"

"Wylie, it's not as simple as that, and you know it."

"Something needs to be done," Wylie stated simply, wondering if killing someone would disrupt the balance of good and evil.

"I agree, but there are other matters at hand. First, we need to find you a place to live, at least for the time being. You're in my employ; you can stay in the servant's house. Would that do for now? Until we can figure out a solution?"

"Adrian, I… I can't." Her shoulders drooped, and she felt his hand on her chin, lifting it so that their eyes met.

"Why? Because of this?" He kissed her lips, and her heart fluttered excitedly.

"Definitely that! What are you doing?"

"Promising you that we are going to figure a way out of this," he answered.

"Well, that takes care of me, but what about my friends? Their families? Their children?" she pushed.

"I will talk to them, tell them to move their things here temporarily until Lord Jameston can be dealt with properly. I will see to it myself, even if it means that I lose everything. Surely he won't make us marry if I'm penniless," he joked.

"Why can't you just break it off, Adrian? Why even go through with it at all. You both love someone else? Why not just break it off?"

"Because if I break it off, it will harm Judith's reputation... Don't you see... money, life, Dobbinsturn...? It's all reputation and purse strings. Politicians are the same. Speaking of which, Lord Jameston may not have told you who his business partners are, but one of them is a high official in the Queen's court. Apparently, he and Jameston are good friends, and he is doing this as a personal favor to the man."

"Adrian, how do you know this?"

"Wylie, the man and I are about to be family... he tells me all sorts of things."

"Then I take it that Judith has not told him about you and me, at least?" Wylie's eyebrows creased in worry.

"You have nothing to worry about. Even Judith isn't that rebellious. Though I would love to see the look on her father's face if she did tell him such a thing. He might have my head for a wall decoration though." He laughed it off, but she couldn't join him in his merriment.

She stepped closer to him, feeling bad for her reaction moments ago.

"I... I do love you. I just don't see how this is all going to work out."

"Nor do I, my love. Lord Jameston and his backers are too rich and influential for us to fight. Perhaps I'll just sell everything and buy an airship so you and I can sail away together." His face grew whimsical, and she longed to grab hold of his dream and make it come true.

Suddenly Wylie had another thought. There was more than one reason the dream could never happen. He must never know that she was a Teselym. The hope of a future together quickly faded as she realized that she would never have a normal life.

"Oh, Adrian. So many things I want to tell you but can't." She wrapped her arms around his neck and buried her face in his shoulder, taking in a deep breath of his soft lavender scent.

"What can't you tell me?" She raised her head to gaze into his face as his arms made their way warmly around her corseted waist.

"Why the dark circles, Adrian? You look as if you haven't slept for some time." The poor man had rings around his eyes as if he hadn't been to bed in a week. He shrugged his shoulders. "Honestly, I sleep at night, but I always feel so tired when I wake. It's as if I haven't slept at all. I imagine my mind is still grieving the loss of my father. Truthfully, though, it's not just his death. There has been a string of deaths as of late. All unexplained, animal attacks people say, but what kind of animal just kills people and leaves them there?" Adrian's face grew sad.

"A good airship Captain friend of ours was the first to go, weeks ago. In fact, right around the time your father died. We didn't hear of it until recently. Apparently, it happened outside a tavern that Judith's father has a stake in, or it's named after him or some such tripe."

Wylie sucked in a deep breath. Deaths around the area? Adrian looks as if he hasn't slept? No… No! Say it isn't so! She screamed mentally, dropping her hands from his shoulders.

"I, I…" She couldn't finish her sentence and instead took off running towards home.

"Wylie," he yelled after her, but she didn't turn around; she just kept running. Things were about to get worse, and fast.

CHAPTER FOURTEEN

Wylie didn't stop, she didn't think, she didn't do anything but hurry until she burst in the door of her home and locked it behind her.

"Please." She yelled at the ceiling, hoping the gods would hear her. "Please. Anyone but Lord Adrian. Please!" She screamed and begged for a long while, crying until she couldn't cry anymore, before crawling into bed to sleep.

Upon awakening, the stark realization that she was losing everything and everyone she loved would have to wait for the moment as she remembered her responsibility to the world. She fished in her side pocket for the Dracosinum and held it gently in her hand. For whatever reason, it was the only thing that made sense to her anymore.

She pressed the fob, and dragon wing cover opened, the little clicks made a comforting sound as Quincy stretched and yawned. His eyes fluttered open sleepily.

"Quincy, I need you. Wake up!"

He smacked his lips together noisily. "I'm awake. I'm awake. Ready for another big night?"

"No, I have questions," she demanded.

"All right, all right… no need to get snippety. I'll answer the best I can."

"Good. You know the Siapheg, correct?"

"I know of it, yes."

"Do you know who it is?"

"Well, of course, I know who it is," he said grumpily.

"Then tell me! I must know because I really can't take the suspense anymore."

"Oh dear, Wylie. I know you have been through quite a lot, but please trust me when I say you do not want to know who it is."

"What is that supposed to mean? If anything, it further confirms my fears!" She shouted, "Why can't you tell me?"

"That would upset the balance, and you know it."

"Tell me how in the names of the gods that would upset the balance? I already have you. Isn't that an upset to the balance?" she shouted at the little beast.

"No Wylie, it's not. I am a moral compass so to speak because you are innately a selfish creature. What I do is help you to not be so selfish. I am able to see situations where your help is needed, which is not something you would see on your own. Don't be angry. Most people don't see how innately selfish they are, and how they could do so much more for people than they do. Most people are so caught up in their own petty little worries that the farthest they get in life is meeting their own needs. They never get to see how rewarding it can be to take care of the needs of others."

Wylie huffed at his response.

"Well, you needn't get mad at that, dear girl. It's not personal. You just need to be taught another way as do most of your kind."

"Then please, answer me this… does that person know yet? Do they know they are the Siapheg?"

"Now that, I can answer honestly… No, to be fair… they do not know who they are yet. They are where you were when your father died."

Wylie breathed a deep sigh of relief. If Lord Adrian was the Siapheg and was flying around killing people at night for whatever reason, at least he didn't know that he was doing it. She had to put a stop to it.

The gears of her mind began turning as she tried to remember if there was anything in the journal about trapping a Dragaleth essence. Perhaps an herbal mixture that would render the human powerless? I don't recall reading such a thing. What if I trap the human and have someone willing to help me trap the dragon form once his essence begins to transform?

It was risky telling anyone of the Dragaleth, but it was crucial to mankind that she put a stop to the Siapheg, especially if it was indeed Lord Adrian. It would require a fair bit of planning since the Siapheg can change sizes. However, if I am right there, watching him change, I can throw chains over it, or a rope or something, immediately.

"I know what you're thinking, and you can't. You can't chain up the Siapheg, or anyone for that matter. It isn't right," Quincy scolded her.

"I hate when you do that," she mumbled, referring to his ability to read her thoughts.

"I know you do, but nonetheless, it is necessary. Come now, we have work to do," he prodded her.

"The hell we do, Quincy. I've got to figure out a way to rescue the people of Lugwallow. That immoral beast of a man, Lord Jameston, has just cut our time even shorter. We have two days to move. It's not enough time!" She paced back and forth, her feet stomping heavily across the floor.

"Wylie, I urge you... look at your Dracosinum. It's near 'The Time of the Dragon'... there is nothing you can do about that problem right now, but there are people even at this moment in need of your help. Please, put aside your human sorrows for a while, and let's save the world. I assure you, all your problems will still be here when we get back." He paced back and forth on the face of the Dracosinum.

"Quincy, there has to be another way. Have the gods not tried to figure out another way to balance good and evil during the night?"

"Why fix what isn't broken?" he countered.

"Why indeed?" she spat back. "Obviously, something is broken, we've never had 'animal attacks' before. But suddenly they're happening with regularity? What do you make of that?"

"I only know what I know. We do not know why the Siapheg has suddenly started killing people. He or she has always feasted on livestock before now. As I said before, it's one of the most level-headed Siapheg I've dealt with for centuries."

"Simply impossible!" she yelled at him. Though it would stand to reason if Lord Adrian were the Siapheg as she assumed, that he would most likely be level-headed. Even if he didn't know what he was doing. Only, that didn't make sense, because his father would have been the Siapheg up until a few days before. Lord McCollum had been gone less than a week which meant Adrian would have been Siapheg for less than a week.

From the sound of it, the attacks had begun right before her father died. Which meant what, exactly? She lifted the Dracosinum to her face and stared Quincy straight in his beady little dragon eyes.

"Quincy, please. People are in danger. I need to stop the Siapheg, and to do that I need to know who he or she is."

"You're finding them is not a moral question. Only their actions are moral actions. I'm sorry, but I simply cannot tell you even if I wanted to. The gods have limited my passing on of knowledge," he continued mouthing words at her, but nothing came out clear.

"What are you doing? Are you quite all right?" she asked.

"Yes, I'm fine. I'm simply demonstrating what happens when I try to share something I'm not permitted to share. My speech becomes mute. My mouth can't even form the words. So, you see, I am not trying to hide anything from you, I just can't say anything regarding the Siapheg unless it is historical knowledge. You have my sincerest apologies, madam." Quincy bowed, sincere sorrow evident on his scale-covered face.

"That is the most preposterous thing I have ever heard! The gods would give me an enemy, but not reveal him or her to me? They would forbid me from knowing who it is?! Tell me how that bloody well makes sense?" She stomped into the living room, grabbing an apple from the kitchen to snack on.

Quincy fluttered after her, the sound of his tiny wings like little gears spinning around inside like a clockwork mouse. He landed on the counter she'd grabbed the fruit from.

"I know it is difficult to understand. I'm not pretending it's not. But I beg of you, leave it till tomorrow. We have much to do this night, I assure you."

She studied him carefully, her eyes watching his wings with increased curiosity until she reached over and picked him up from the counter. "Quincy!" she exclaimed, noticing for the first time that under the layers of scales, and iridescent green, his wings attached to his body at pivot points that were made of the tiniest of gears and springs. "Spread your wings, please?" He did as he was asked, and she gasped in amazement. Every limb was connected by rods and pinions. She ran to the tiny mirrored vanity bench near the door and grabbed a magnifying glass from its compartment.

Holding it up to her face, she spent a great deal of time stroking his scales and poking at his tail.

"Why Quincy! You're made entirely of clock parts!"

"Yes, ma'am."

"Why didn't I see it before?"

"Well, Miss Wylie... as I mentioned, you had to come into the knowledge of who you are and who you are meant to be before you could see the truth. It works in a similar way with me. As you accept your purpose, you will begin to see things for how they really are. It will be as if blinders have fallen from your eyes. The longer you are a Teselym, the more it will affect you on a daily basis.

"Your human mind will be unable to forget truth once it experiences it first-hand. What you may not realize at this moment, is that these are not scales, they too are tiny gears and cogs that make up my form. It is why I never get tired and never need to eat. You see, my dear. I am made entirely of watch parts. A reminder that we are living on borrowed time, and that we only have mere moments to stop evil when it occurs."

"Another gift from the gods to me, so that I, just like you, never forget my place," Wylie said.

His form became very clear then, and right before her eyes, the iridescent green scales that she had seen before simply disappeared.

"Illusion?" she whispered.

"No. More like… candy coating on your new reality. Other things will be revealed to you over time. Just you wait and see." He grinned broadly, "At least now I know you are seeing me for who I really am." His little bronze body was much less polished than the green scales she had grown accustomed to seeing.

"Don't worry, Wylie. You'll get used to it. I'm amazed it happened so quickly. Your father saw me as a little green beast for months before he finally realized the truth. Not that I fault the guy, he saw the good in everyone. Even when there wasn't good to be seen," Quincy's mouth turned downward, and his eyes fell. "He was a good man, was your father. The world is a lonelier place without him."

"I take it you two were more than just Teselym and moral compass?" she asked softly.

"Most definitely, my dear Wylie. He was an awfully good man, and the closest to a friend my little clockwork body has known in years." Quincy brushed at his eyes quickly and then stood tall. "Never mind that. We have work to do." He was all business now, and Wylie dared not ruin the moment. So, she transformed herself into the smallest of dragon forms and snuck out the mouse hole into the street again before taking to the skies.

She smelled it before she saw it, and as she rose into the sky, the Siapheg swirled below her. Unaware of her presence, it seemed to be looking for something on the streets below. She followed it for a brief while, and soon enough, she saw a young woman walking alone. The Siapheg saw her too and steeled itself before arching its back ready to spring. Wylie knew it was going in for the kill.

She swooped down, throwing her body against the black scaled beast, her nemesis. It fell to the ground, hitting the stones with a tremendous thud. The woman with her unkempt bloomers and crooked corset, a sign that she had been up to no good, took off running, the sounds of her high-pitched screams echoing into the night. Harlot or not, it didn't mean she deserved to die.

The Siapheg got up from the ground and charged at Wylie. Its dark brown eyes struck her with a familiarity that Wylie had feared. Her heart sank. He would not remember this, tomorrow when he awoke, but she would. How could she bring herself to fight the one she loved?

"Just do what is right," Quincy interrupted her thoughts.

"Of course, you have something to…." The Siapheg's head rammed her hard in the side, knocking the breath out of her. Her body began careening toward the ground just as he had done moments before. She managed to catch her balance before she slammed into the ground. Flapping her wings madly, she rose back into the sky. The Siapheg flew straight at her once more.

Wylie got a sudden flash of a little girl in a run-down home, an angry drunken man standing threateningly over the cowering form of a blonde-haired child. Wylie quickly grabbed her Dracosinum and felt the tingle as she was transported instantly to the scene. When she opened her eyes, she saw a wood-slatted house and heard the muffled yells of a drunk man inside. The sounds of a woman sobbing and a little girl crying could be heard through the dilapidated wooden door.

"Charlie, please... don't take it out on her. I don't know where the rent money has gone, but please... she is only a child!" The man called Charlie muttered a string of obscenities, then something hit the wall with a shattering sound.

The Teselym part of Wylie took over, and without thinking about it, she smashed open the door, seized the woman and child in her powerful jaws, and carried them gently out of the house, whipping the man viciously with her powerful tail as she left the pathetic hovel.

Wylie flew over the city until she came to a convent known for protecting battered women and children. Gently depositing mother and child on the ground, she whispered, "Tell no one what you've seen, just start over and give this little girl the life she deserves." Even as Wylie spoke, she could make out the bruises on the little girl's face and arms. The mother, clinging to the child, nodded her head as Wylie continued, "This place will take care of you. You must simply be straightforward about what your husband has done to you." The woman bowed her head in thanks. Moments later Wylie's Dracosinum transported her to the next location.

Her disappearance was like something from a glorious dream that folk would subsequently characterize as mystical and surreal.

It proved to a long night for Wylie, with many wrongs righted and justice meted out, but finally it was time to return to Lugwallow. As she neared her home, she searched the streets and skies with apprehension.

"Tell me, Quincy, has anyone been killed by the Siapheg tonight?"

"Not as yet, Miss. Safe to say you should be returning home before sunrise. The 'Time of the Dragon' draws to an end."

"Very well," and she flew silently home, all the while struggling to come up with a plan to prevent her beloved from perpetrating the evil he would no doubt wreak upon London, and indeed many parts of the world. The thought saddened her, but it felt like this was the way things were meant to be. It was just her lousy luck that she would fall for the one man that was her exact opposite in all the worst ways.

CHAPTER FIFTEEN

As Wylie arrived home and shrank in size, Quincy exited the Dracosinum and flitted about the room, finally coming to land on her father's bed.

Lord Adrian is the Siapheg… I just know it… What will I do? How will I stop him? Wylie's thoughts were growing louder and more insistent now that she was home.

"Do not fret about that." Quincy tried to ease her worries.

"Quincy, how can I not? You won't tell me if my worst fears are confirmed. I don't know what else to do but worry."

"My dear, nothing is ever as it seems. You know that much…" she nodded agreement to his statement. "Now, if you don't mind, Wylie girl. I'm going to take a long soak in a warm thimbleful of oil." Wylie nodded again as her Teselym form dissipated and her essence reentered her human body.

She felt as if her human form still wanted to sleep, but there was so much to be done. She fully intended to help the people of Lugwallow pack up their things, but where would they go? Some of them had several children and the Widow Turpin was elderly, so being uprooted wouldn't do her any good at all. It was going to be more stressful to handle than she had intended.

"Well, Wylie? What are you going to do?" she asked herself out loud. If only I could use my Teselym strengths to my advantage. She would gladly grab the people up one by one and take them somewhere lovely, like a castle in Ireland... where they would all stay together and be safe until she figured out what to do with the horrible man who happened to be her best friend's father.

She suddenly wished she had asked Quincy about using her powers in such a way, but she was reluctant to disturb him in his oil soak. Nonsense, I can figure this out on my own. Reason told her that technically if she were helping her people, it was still balancing good and evil; she would be doing good for an entire parish full of people who were being cast out. What was nobler than that? Then again, doing away with the hateful Lord Jameston seemed entirely feasible too, but she was pretty sure Quincy would frown on her murdering anyone.

She rushed over to the Widow Turpin's home, banging loudly on her door.

"Widow Turpin, it's me… please… open up."

"All right, all right… hold your horses. I'm coming, I'm coming." The door squeaked open, and Wylie noticed that there were three carpet bags full to the brim sitting to one side. She rushed forward, throwing her arms around the widow. "I can't believe they'll be here tomorrow!" She had fought hard to be brave, but it was difficult to be strong when she felt as if she had nothing left to hold onto.

"I know, child. Why aren't you packing?" The widow hugged her back, but it was awkward at best. They had never been close, and now they had been thrust into a difficult situation.

"I'm already packed," Wylie said softly before stepping away.

"The police, Lord Jameston's men, they're all going to be here in the morning, we should get everyone out of here tonight."

"Surely he will toss us out quick as look at us. He is a much crueler man than I ever imagined," the widow said, her eyes full to the brim with tears.

"No sense lollygagging around dear, why don't you go check on the others? Make sure they're ready to go so we can be out of here tonight. Shout it from the streets if you must, we've no time to waste."

Wylie nodded, running outside, her voice raised in fervor.

"People! Good People of Lugwallow! It's time to slumber no longer! You must be out by tonight! For tomorrow he will come to take us from our homes and send us to jail! Please, hurry!" She ran up and down the street, knocking on doors. Her pleas met with grumbling and protests of unfairness

"Please, I know it's not right. I assure you I am working on a solution to the problem, but until there is one, we need to pack our things and get out. He will be here tomorrow." Wylie's urgency prodded everyone into action. The urgency in her voice made the dire situation all the more real as they struggled to gather together their meager belongings and children and stand on the street.

"Wylie? What are we to do!? Where are we to go?" The Riverpont family had the most children of everyone in Lugwallow, and as all eight of them ran around outside, laughing and chasing one another, their mother Hannah cried for what she was losing.

"Hannah, I am not entirely sure. I have a friend who might be able to help us. Let everyone know I'll be back as soon as I can!" Running back to her house Wylie snatched up her derringer and tucked it in its pouch at her side. She pulled the Dracosinum out its pocket.

"Quincy, I know you're not sleeping. Now that I know what you are."

"Very well," he said, as she opened the device. "What is it, child?"

"I need to transport somewhere now. I am out of time."

"What are you asking me for?" he snapped.

"Huh?"

"Well, you're a grown woman and a grown Dragaleth. Use your powers as you must, you don't answer to me."

"Well, won't the gods smite me down with thunderbolts and lightning and all that?" she asked.

"My heavens no. As long as what you do falls in line with your duties as a Teselym, they are your powers to command. The only limitations are 'The Time of the Dragon.' Which starts anywhere after the sixth hour of the evening and ends at the sixth hour of the morning. The sixth hour of the morning is the only hour set in stone." His little brass body whirred and clicked as he marched around on the Dracosinum.

"So, what about transporting a load of people to a safe place nearby where they can rest until they are allowed to move back into their homes?"

"No can do, my dear. I'm afraid the Dracosinum is for your use only."

"Very well, better tuck back in. I've somewhere to be," she stated matter-of-factly.

"Aye, madam." Quincy laid down inside the Dracosinum, and she snapped it shut, gripped it firmly, and visualized the stables of her employer Lord Adrian. He may be the Siapheg, but he doesn't know it yet, and until he does, he may be of some use to me.

When she opened her eyes, Chaos was looking curiously at her and stamping his hooves, almost as if to protest her sudden appearance.

"Relax, Chaos. All is well. Is your master about?" Chaos whinnied enthusiastically, and she rubbed his velvet nose, kissing him before she ran out of the stable and up to the house.

"Lord Adrian! Lord Adrian!" She banged on the door furiously.

It opened to reveal a very irate looking Hettie, the same housemaid that had heard Wylie proclaim that she would like to murder Lord Jameston. The maid looked quite frightened, and ran off, calling over her shoulder, "I'll find his Lordship." She sounded a bit out of breath, but Wylie didn't care.

"Lord Adrian, please! Are you home?" She yelled loudly into the house. To her left, the shuffling of feet warned her that someone was approaching.

Lord Adrian in a white long-sleeved shirt, top buttons undone, emerged from the parlor, his face a mixture of emotions which she was unable to read.

"Lord Adrian!" she exclaimed.

"W... W... Wylie..." he stuttered, his dark hair unkempt, and his hands fumbling to clasp the cufflinks at his wrists. "What... what is it? Have you changed your mind?"

"Changed my mind about what?"

"About us?" he asked, his eyes earnest and dare she think it? Hopeful.

"Oh, Adrian. Please don't make this difficult for me." Her mind flashed back to the Siapheg form, black as a crow as it swooped down on the harlot he most certainly would have killed had she not intervened. "I can't even think about that right now, please… I've come for something else."

He finished fastening his cuffs, and shrugged on his vest, while she spoke.

"Yes, well, what is it?"

"I am about to ask you a huge favor. I know it's an imposition, but I don't know who else to turn to."

"Out with it, Wyles." He buttoned the two buttons concealing the tanned skin of his arms. She followed him about as he dressed, but when he headed towards the bedroom, she hung back. "Don't be silly; I am only going to comb my hair." She leaned on the door frame while he stood in front of the wash basin and mirror in his room. He applied a dollop of Macassar Oil to his hair, then ran the comb through it until his hair had a slick, clean shine to it. Exiting his room, he made his way to the front door. Grabbing his top hat from the hat rack, he popped it onto his head and patted it into place.

"Please, Adrian. Everyone in Lugwallow has been cast out of their homes. Those families... they have children… pets… personal belongings. They're going to lose everything. I've come to ask if you can suggest a way to shelter these people for a few days until they can get their affairs in order. I just don't want them on the street."

Adrian stopped for a moment and turned to face her. She could tell by his expression that he was deep in thought.

"Wylie, did we not just speak of this before?" Wylie felt confused. He paced back and forth for a minute, stroking his chin before he quite suddenly grabbed a long black duster that she had never seen him wear before. "Aha!" he said, still not answering her question, or explaining what he meant by his statement moments before. He held out his arm to her, and she put her arm through his.

"Come, I have something to show you." He winked mischievously, and once again, she noticed the dark circles under his eyes. They had grown, and she wondered why she wasn't suffering from the same affliction. Her human body seemed well rested each morning when she returned from her Teselym duties.

"What is it?"

"Don't you worry yourself. I have this all figured out. Your timing is perfect!" His eyes glowed with excitement. She hurried along with him as they rushed outside where he bypassed the carriages in the driveway. "Come, come..." He led her towards the servant's house, a large, elaborate building, smaller in size, but almost as lovely as the main house itself.

"Why are we going to the servant's house?"

"This isn't the servant's house," he stated simply, "The servant's house is over there." He waved his hand towards a building near the rear of the property. She had seen it before but had just assumed it was the carriage house. Lord Adrian opened a pair of large doors, and as she followed him inside, she realized she had been wrong.

The elaborate building he had brought her to, had luxurious cherry wood floors and large high ceilinged rooms. From what she could see there were numerous workbenches covered with tools of every description. She now realized what she had always thought to be the servant's house was actually a carriage house. It would easily hold two or three large carriages, but instead only contained one large carriage-shaped object with a heavy dust cloth over it.

"A carriage house?" she ventured.

"Yes!" he nodded, a boyish smile spreading across his mischievous face. "Wait 'til you see what I've made!" He grabbed the dust cloth and pulled it back revealing a huge gleaming carriage.

"I don't understand. What's the big deal? It looks like a fancier version of the two carriages you already own. The ones sitting outside there lacking proper care." She spoke with an air of irritation, but her tone went right over his head.

"Yes, my dear, but looks can be deceiving. I'll show you the inside in a moment, but first, we need to light the fire. Follow me." Lord Adrian went to the rear of the carriage and opened a steel door. Wylie saw that a wood fire had already been laid in the grate, complete with kindling and some crumpled paper. Lord Adrian struck a wooden sulfur match on the door and touched the flame to the paper, which immediately flared up.

"Now, while the boiler is heating up, come take a look at the interior." He opened the large double wooden doors on the side of the carriage. They reminded her very much of the double doors on a tavern that swing back and forth. As they climbed up into the spacious seating area, she immediately noticed a panel with many dials and levers mounted at the front. This certainly was no ordinary carriage.

Lord Adrian grasped a T-shaped handle and began pumping furiously, which set off whirring and grinding sounds from the rear of the carriage.

She couldn't see what was happening, but she heard the cranking. Then he grasped another handle on the opposite side and did the same thing. The carriage was starting to make strange noises and vibrate slightly as if it were coming to life.

"What do you say, Wylie, shall we take a ride? We can transport the people of Lugwallow here more quickly. As I told you just yesterday, your friends and the people of Lugwallow Parish are welcome to stay here. With the carriage empty, they can load up, and I'll bring them back here, though it will take numerous trips." He smiled triumphantly, pumping his fist in the air, while the steam made fizzing and spitting sounds beneath them. It was quite noisy, and she yelled back.

"You meant all of them, the people too? When you said 'bring their things here temporarily' I thought you meant just that, just their things. I didn't think you were considering them too." Her eyes welled up at his generosity.

"Wylie, you must know by now that I would do anything for your happiness. Now come, we've much to do, and this will help us." He waved his hand gallantly over his contraption.

"What in the world is this thing?" she asked, as she wiped a tear away, still slightly overcome with emotion.

"Well, it's a horse-drawn carriage without the horses. Have a seat, and I'll explain it to you on our way to Lugwallow." His eyes sparkled with delight, and she delighted in his excitement.

"Fine, fine, is this thing safe?"

"I don't honestly know." He laughed, and reaching his hand out to her, pulled her down to the seat beside him. There were levers and buttons and gleaming dials in front of her, but for the life of her, she had no idea what they were for.

"Well, you see Wylie… it's like this." He flipped a small lever and pressed his foot down on a pedal on the floor. The carriage began to creep forward slowly. "Newton's law of motion states that an object in motion stays in motion, you know… unless something stops it. So, my thought process was, what must I do to get an object of this mass to move forward, accelerate, and stay in motion?"

The carriage began to move more quickly as they headed toward Lugwallow, and Wylie couldn't help but notice the astounded looks from passersby as they rolled down the street.

"Uh huh." She was a bit astounded herself and had a hard time trying to think of anything intelligent to say.

"So I surmised that a steam engine would create enough inertia to propel this form of transportation forward and allow me to keep it going. It's quite intricate, but I simply installed a firebox and a boiler. I have to start the fire first before I take off and allow it time to heat the boiler, but it takes very little effort to do so. The boiler is located at the back, underneath the carriage itself. For short distances, at least, it should be quite safe.

"The water goes into the boiler through a filler pipe on the back. This dial shows the water level. A float in the water tank is connected to this gauge and tells me the water level. When it gets to this mark, it needs to be refilled.

"The steam created in the boiler activates the pistons which are attached to the rear wheels and gets them going. This little set of dials here shows me the temperature and steam pressure. I can adjust both by moving this lever here. Everything is measured with precision, and once I get the wheels turning, it requires less steam pressure to keep them moving."

"And you did this? All by yourself?"

"Aye. That I did!" He smiled broadly at her, before turning to wave at gawkers. He turned the steam knob, causing the steam-carriage to go faster. "Let's hurry along, shall we?"

"What happens when you go too fast? Or need to stop? Or run out of water or steam or any number of things?"

"Well, it's not perfected yet, but that's exactly why I said I couldn't take it long distances. There is a wood box where I can store extra wood beneath the undercarriage. As for the water, there's another tank back there.

"I started building this before my father died, but with him gone, and my inability to sleep, I've spent a lot of time working on it. I completed it last night. Never got a wink of sleep, but it doesn't matter. I finished it," he yelled out jubilantly.

"It is truly and utterly amazing, Adrian. You are a remarkable man." If he was up all night building this thing, that means he can't possibly be the Siapheg. And that means the Siapheg is still at large. "Dang Blammit," she said aloud.

"I beg your pardon?"

"Oh nothing, I'm sorry Adrian. I'm just worried about the parish of Lugwallow."

"Well, don't you worry, I have more than enough rooms in my house and servants quarters to shelter them for a few nights. That ought to really ruffle Lord Jameston's feathers."

"What? Adrian, you can't do that."

"Oh, but yes, I can. And I will. Lady Judith will think it's a hoot." He tossed his head back and laughed as his steam-powered carriage rolled into Lugwallow. Many of the people were standing outside, their bags and personal effects piled around them. The carriage started to slow as Lord Adrian pulled on a tall lever mounted on the floor. Finally, the carriage came to a stop, wheezing and puffing, amid clouds of steam.

"Get them loaded up Wylie, let's get them back to my house before nightfall. It will take several trips before we get them all." Wiley didn't even question him anymore; she simply nodded and rounded up the Riverpont family as they had the most children.

"Hannah, Jonathan… come now… you can trust Lord Adrian. He wants to help us. Load up your things and go with him to his home. He's going to take us all in for a few days until we can figure out what to do about Lord Jameston." Hannah started to protest, but Jonathan wrapped a caring arm around her.

"It will be all right, Hannah. Come on, children, let's go!" he called out to them. Wylie helped lift them up into the carriage, and Jonathan sat up front with Adrian, to make room for the children in the back with their mother.

"Wylie, why don't you get yourself packed. I'll be back soon, okay?" She nodded to Adrian, bewildered by the turn of events. How was she going to be the Teselym without being caught now? Living in a house full of people was a good way to get seen coming and going, or even worse, what if someone walked in on her in the middle of her transformation or tried to check on her 'sleeping' body?

Calm down, Wylie. You're getting ahead of yourself. She watched anxiously as the steam-powered carriage rolled out of sight. Her things had been packed for days, after all, what more would she need but her clothes? Furniture was replaceable. Except for the few pieces her father had built.

If all went well, she would be back in her home within a few days. Surely once Lord Jameston saw that Lord Adrian intended to allow the residents of Lugwallow to live in his house, he would have to change his mind if only to spare Judith. Wylie could only hope for positive results at the moment.

True to his word, Adrian made several trips and retrieved the families one by one, until it was nearly pitch dark outside. She knew it was well past her time to transform, so when he made one last trip to pick her up, along with the three remaining people, an elderly couple and their grandson, she declined.

"I'll join you in the morning, Adrian. I have some last-minute things to take care of here. At least for now, my townspeople are safe. I can sleep peacefully tonight."

"No, Wylie. You must come! Lord Jameston's men will be here tomorrow with the police, and they will take you away if they catch you here."

"Don't worry Adrian. Here…" She threw her carpetbag up into the carriage. "There, that's all I need. I'll be at your house first thing in the morning, I promise. I just want to take care of a few small things here. I won't get caught, I promise."

"Are you sure?"

"I'm certain." She smiled at him, the soft streetlamp now shining over them.

"All right, be safe." He reached down from the carriage door, grabbed her hand, and pulled her close to kiss her on the forehead. "If all goes well, perhaps we will be able to be together when this is all over." Gasps and exclamations came from within the carriage.

"That isn't going over well." She laughed. "I'm sure the widow Turpin will have a heyday with that." She let out an exasperated sigh.

"So let her. I'll take good care of your people, love. You take care of yourself, and I'll see you soon."

"That you will, Adrian. That you will."

He nodded at her, released the brake, and flipped the steam switch propelling the carriage forward, and the last of Lugwallow's inhabitants disappeared into the night.

Wylie ran into her house, quickly changed into her nightdress, crawled under the covers, and opened the Dracosinum. The tiny blue flame rose from her chest, and as her own body lost consciousness, the Teselym body formed around her essence and she quickly rose through the open window and took to the sky.

Wylie threw herself into her night's work, listening intently to the directions and promptings that sprang up in her mind. Even Quincy could sense that she meant business, and he stayed quiet most of the night, except to give her guidance a time or two or to help her decide which cases were most urgent.

"It's hard to believe so much evil goes on at night, Quincy."

"Yes, well, even more goes on in the daylight, right underneath our very noses," he answered back.

"Why do I never feel tired?" the thought struck her.

"You are… how shall we say…" his little cogs whirring and clicking softly. "You are Teselym-powered now. You require much less sleep because you are part god. The tiniest part of a god. Their tears. It is enough to give you incredible strength, speed, sharper judgment, and so much more. So far, you've only just scratched the surface of your possibilities as a Teselym. Using them in your human form makes you more Teselym than human. Now that you've united the two, you'll find that you will only sleep if you want to. It's going to be a matter of choice, honestly."

"Hmm," she mumbled as she flew over her last city of the night before heading home. She could see the slight hint of the sun coming up, meaning 'The Time of the Dragon' was up. She transported home, transformed back into her own body, donned her clothes, and then transported to Lord Adrian's stable. Feeling that it would be less conspicuous for her to be seen coming from there.

Now all we have to do is wait.

CHAPTER SIXTEEN

Wylie rapped gently on the door, knowing it was still quite early, and she would be lucky if anyone were awake at this hour. The door whipped open before she had finished knocking, and Adrian grabbed her hand, yanked her inside, and into his arms.

The soft musky lavender scent that was Adrian was like a salve to an open wound she had no idea she had been trying to conceal. The moment he held her, her legs went weak beneath her. Hot tears streamed silently down her cheeks.

"I'm so glad you're all right. I was sure that Lord Jameston had already tossed you in jail and thrown away the key."

"After what we've done, I wouldn't put it past him," she replied weakly.

"My love, are you okay?" he whispered softly into her ear.

"Oh, Adrian… I'm just overwhelmed and so tired." She feigned a yawn.

"I know, love," he said as he stroked her hair. "It's all going to be okay."

"He's going to ruin you, you know," she said.

"Let him. He can't do anything to me." Adrian was so sure about the situation. As if the devil himself had heard the conversation, a sudden loud banging came at the front door. Adrian gently pushed Wylie behind him. "Well, well… our friend got here early, just as I assumed." Some of the people had started to wake up and come down the stairs.

Wylie could tell they were worried. The banging sounded again.

"Lord Adrian, I know you're in there! I have received word of your shenanigans! Open the door."

Lord Adrian spoke to the group, "Don't worry. I've already requested the cooks make a large breakfast this morning. We will be eating shortly. In the meantime, worry not. You are all free to shower and use my home as if it were your own. Once I've dealt with Lord Jameston, we'll sit down together and celebrate our victory, all right?" Some of them nodded half-heartedly in response. The rest rather dubious moved off toward the good smells coming from the kitchen.

Lord Adrian grabbed Wylie's hand, pulling her gently along behind him, then pushed her out of sight behind him as he opened the door.

"Well, good morning, Lord Jameston. So happy to see you arrived back from your little venture out of town yesterday." Lady Judith appeared at her father's side. "I trust all went well?"

"Yes, until I arrived back in town last night and heard something that quite disturbed me," he hissed through clenched teeth.

"Oh? And just what might possibly upset the unflappable Lord Jameston?" Adrian quipped.

"I got wind that you ... you…" Lord Jameston's face turned several shades of red before he spat out the words, "You are housing the people of Lugwallow!"

At those words, Lord Adrian pulled Wylie from behind him and held her tightly to his side. He flung the door wide so that Lord Jameston was able to see the people gathered behind him listening to the confrontation.

"Those reports would be correct. See, I heard tell that a villainous man, concerned only with his own welfare rather than that of innocent men, women, and children, had bought all of Lugwallow and wanted the parish emptied within two days. Well, I, being a concerned and compassionate citizen, could not very well allow my fellow humans to be tossed out on the street as if they were nothing more than vermin. So, I invited them to come stay with me until we were able to sort this whole mess out," Adrian finished with a wide smile. Wylie was worried that Judith would be angry but was surprised to see her stifling a giggle. Her large emerald eyes sparkled with laughter.

"You will rue the day you crossed me, Lord Adrian. You and that worthless gutter rat will both regret it. The wedding is off. I will not have my beautiful daughter marrying someone who collects so much... trash." Lord Jameston looked Wylie up and down before turning abruptly and yanking his daughter along with him.

"Father, you can't treat me this way!"

"Shut up, girl." He smacked her across the face, and Wylie broke free from Adrian and went after Lord Jameston.

"How dare you treat her in such a way?" she hollered, and as he turned to face her, his mouth open to say something, she punched him square in the jaw.

"Why you insolent…" She hit him again and would have continued doing so, but Lord Adrian had rushed to her side and held her arm back from the third swing.

"Wylie! Stop! You cannot act in such a way!"

"I will. He is not a human being with actual feelings. He deserves that and more." She wriggled out of his clutches and went after Jameston again who was preparing to hit her back. He balled his fist up, but before he could land a punch, Wylie's foot flew up and caught him squarely between the legs causing him to bend forward gasping in pain. Both hands held onto his codpiece which apparently had provided little protection. As he fell forward onto his knees in pain, something shiny slipped from the pocket of his waistcoat and rolled silently into the grass beside the walkway.

"You... will… pay… for… that..." he said through clenched teeth, puffing like a steam engine as he finally gathered himself off the ground, hobbled back to his carriage, and climbed painfully inside. She laughed giddily as he disappeared.

"Oh Wylie, what have you done?" Adrian's face had drained of all color, but the others who had come to watch whooped and hollered in delight, cheering her for what she had done.

"Never you mind," she said to him. "There is nothing he can do to me; he isn't as great as he thinks he is. It's about time someone put him in his place." She turned away then and went to pick up the item that had dropped to the ground.

"I agree with you, Wylie." Lady Judith nodded her head and followed after her. "Except you have injured the one thing that is more important to him than any of his possessions, and that is his pride. He will be out for blood."

"Oh, I have no doubt…" Wylie stopped mid-sentence as she examined the item that had dropped from his waistcoat. A bronze item, very much like a pocket watch, with an intricate dragon design on the front of it. She let out an audible gasp and turned to face Judith.

"Judith… Do… do you know what this is?"

"Yes! It's a very fancy pocket watch. My father carries it with him always. It's an heirloom that has been passed down through his family. He never lets it out of his sight," she explained.

"It's your father's?" An idea was forming in Wylie's mind. If Lord Jameston was the Siapheg, as this Dracosinum she was holding suggested, then she would fight him to the death. Killing him would upset the balance of good and evil, but fighting the Siapheg would not be against any rules. It was all part of her purpose as the Teselym. The only downside was that if she fought him and he died, then the role of Siapheg would pass to his daughter. That would mean she and Lady Judith would be at odds, not that Judith needed to know that. Perhaps Wylie could take control of the Siapheg's Dracosinum, and prevent Judith from assuming the role.

Wylie needed more time to think her plan through.

"Can I have it please?" Lady Judith asked, holding out her hand. "He's going to have your head as it is if he finds out you have this. He will make you suffer. Please… don't make your punishment any worse than it has to be."

"Sure, no problem." Wylie dropped the Dracosinum in her friend's hand, formulating a plan for how she would sneak it back when Lady Judith wasn't looking or had set it down somewhere.

"Well, we've had quite enough excitement for one day. Shall we have breakfast?" Adrian urged, his face still near colorless.

"Hurrah!" came the cheers from the people of Lugwallow that had watched the entire event with fascination. The lot of them disappeared back inside the house, and Wylie couldn't help noticing that Lord Adrian triple-locked the front door. As if that would stop a man like Lord Jameston if he chose to enter. One swoop of an ax and the locks would give way in short order.

I guess he's allowed his delusions... she thought as they all gathered around the tables in the dining room where steaming plates of food sat waiting. Several shining platters adorned the tables, and all of those present sat down and enjoyed a peaceful meal, eating their fill before the servants came to clear the dishes.

Wylie had not felt such contentment in a long while and being with them reminded her of the meals she'd shared with her father when he was well. She was barely able to remember her mother's face anymore, but she swore that the laughter heard around the table was that of her mom, and not of the Widow Turpin, or Hannah Ravenpont.

It was a brief moment of happiness, but like all good things, it came to an end all too quickly. No sooner had the dishes been cleared than a loud banging came once more at the front door.

"Adrian, you may as well open up, son, and hand over that carcass that is stinking up our lives!" The boom of Lord Jameston's voice could be heard through the door, even over the laughter which stopped quite suddenly.

"Lord Adrian! It's Lord Jameston. He's brought a whole lot of mutton-shunters with him, and they look armed and angry!" timid little housemaid Hettie Davenport spoke excitedly, red-faced and sweating.

"Calm yourself, Hettie. I'll handle this man and his coppers. Thinks he can march up to my house and tell me what to do!" Lord Adrian yanked open the door and leaned against the lintel with as much resolve as a Grenadier guard.

"Well, are you going to hand her over?"

"Um, no… don't think I will." Adrian responded.

"Coppers, seize him. I want him thrown in jail until this can be dealt with."

"Aye, Sir," one of the men stepped forward to grab Adrian's arm, but Wylie ran out of the house, pushing the uniformed man abruptly away.

"It's me you want, you tyrant." she stood in front of him, chest puffed out bravely. She had hidden her derringer in the house to be retrieved later, and her Dracosinum was safely tucked down the front of her corset where she prayed it would remain undetected. 'The Time of the Dragon' was close at hand. As long as they tossed her in a cell and walked away, she'd be gone before they'd figured out exactly what had happened.

She would find Lord Jameston in his Siapheg form that very eve and fight him to the death. It was the only thing she was allowed to do. She was sure Judith would be more just in her dealings, even if she were descended from the same bloodline. Judith had love in her heart, and compassion for people. Wylie would just have to count on that being true, even after Judith learned the truth and transformed. It was the only solution she was able to come up with.

She felt something hard and uncomfortable pressing against her spine.

"Move along, little lady." The copper nudged her with the cold brass of something unforgiving in her back. "One wrong move from you, and me and my newly acquired carbon blaster will knock you from here to kingdom come."

She only nodded in response as she was shoved into the horse-drawn Black Maria police van. Once seated, shackles were fastened around her ankles and wrists to prevent her escape. The arresting officer sat across from her, his odd-shaped gun pointed at her while he smiled a near-toothless smile.

"Will you be joining us, Lord Jameston?" A voice from the front of the cab called out.

"No, Lieutenant Addle. I just ask that she is prevented from bothering me or any of us ever again. I've made my charges against her very clear," Jameston answered.

"Indeed, you have." The lieutenant clicked his tongue, and soon the police carriage was bouncing along. Wylie knew that if she lived to see the daylight of the next day, it would be a miracle. She couldn't waste time once she arrived at the jail, assuming they didn't find her Dracosinum first.

CHAPTER SEVENTEEN

The ride was a long one, and soon Wylie found herself drifting off to sleep with the rocking of the Black Maria. When the carriage finally stopped, the lieutenant himself was prodding her awake. He had a young, lightly-bearded face, but she could not read his eyes, and that was something that bothered her quite a lot.

"Come along, troublemaker. I have a special cell for you." He spoke in low, sinister tones that sent shivers up her spine. There goes any hope of ever getting out of this place alive. The sudden evil she felt radiating off the man made her skin crawl and sent shivers down her spine. Something told her that she would need to deal with him on a more serious level if she was able to gain her Teselym form.

"Oh, joy of joys. I can't wait," she mumbled. He turned around and grabbed her hair, yanking her head back, his slimy voice whispering low into her ear.

"Say another word, gutter rat, and you won't make it through the next few hours alive. Understand?" She could barely move her head, but she mumbled a weak 'yes' as her eyes teared up from the pain of having her hair nearly yanked from her scalp. He followed close behind her and jammed his gun so roughly into her spine, she pictured bruises forming. He nudged her down the stone steps of the jail where the smell of unwashed men, urine, and death invaded her nostrils and burned her eyes.

"See, this here is where I take people to die. I like you though. I think you have some potential, and I happen to think that Lord Jameston is a pretentious chiseler."

Had her situation not been so dire, she would have prattled back to him about all the things that Lord Jameston was full of, for it wasn't just about cheating, as the term 'chiseler' suggested. Lord Jameston was a special breed of man whom, she was convinced, had been born without a heart at all.

The copper shoved his foot into her backside.

"Hurry up, wench. I don't have all day to deal with the likes of you." She felt the Dracosinum shift as he nudged her along. If she sped up anymore, she was afraid it would dislodge from her corset and fall to the damp, dirty floor of the jail.

Men whooped and hollered as she passed by, some of them toothless and with hair so thick with dirt and grease they barely looked human at all.

She couldn't draw her eyes away. She had seen some disheartening things in her short time as a Teselym. But those were things that she had been able to do something about. The smell and the conditions of the men down here was unspeakable. What if, like me, they've been put here unjustifiably?

Mustn't think of that now. The Dracosinum was shifting again, with every step she took it slipped lower. If it fell out, she would never get out of here. Then the cop grabbed her shoulder and halted her in front of a lone cell set apart from the rest. A pile of ragged clothing and a lump of something impossible to identify in the dark were the only contents of the cell. Chain shackles hung from the left wall.

"Get over there," he growled as he opened the steel barred door, and nodded towards the shackles.

"You don't need to chain me up. I'm not going anywhere," she cried out.

"Shut yer mouth." He pointed the pistol at her and cocked the hammer back. She prayed to the gods that the Dracosinum would take on a mind of its own and somehow climb back up her to her chest. *Where is Quincy when I need him?*

The cop unlocked the shackles from her wrists and shoved her towards the wall. The sudden rough movement dislodged the Dracosinum from its place, and she felt the cold brass slide down to the right side of her waist, and then it was gone. She heard the soft thud as it hit the dirt floor.

Acting as if he had shoved her too hard, Wylie fell backward against the wall and slid to the ground, her freed hands searching for the cold brass item in the dim cell.

"Ya clumsy nitwit!" he yelled at her, reaching down to help her up. "Let's get you in these chains." *Come on Wylie! Think of something!*

"Please, please don't chain me up! I beg of you." She teared up.

"Lady, if I don't chain you up and Lord Jameston finds out, it will be me instead of you on the gallows. You sure riled up the wrong man. Now git over there or you won't make it till morning!" He pulled her to a standing position and motioned with the flintlock. Her heart raced as she realized there was no getting out of this situation. She hoped to crawl on the floor and find the blasted device. Once she opened it and assumed her Teselym form, she would deal with this fellow properly.

It's going to take a miracle.

She glanced from him to the chains on the wall, then back to him again. Wylie noticed even in the darkness of the cell, he was staring at her just a little too intensely… or possibly something else... An idea was forming.

"Please... this is possibly my last night, have mercy, m'lord." She pleaded with him, batting her lashes and bowing slightly. She heard the hammer on the flintlock click again. His gaze was locked on her tightly corseted chest. Yep, no mystery there. Disgusted by what she needed to do, she took a small step backward until she was leaning against the damp, cold wall. She thrust her corseted chest outward, her bosom pressing tightly against her buttoned up blouse. Ever modest, she couldn't believe the boundaries she now dared cross to save her own life.

"Lieutenant," she breathed huskily, "I am willing to do what it takes to get out of being chained," she enunciated each word for effect and watched as his face went from intense to lusty-eyed.

"Willing to do what it takes, huh?" He shoved the flintlock in its holster at his side and made his way to her. The smell of sweat and death pervaded her nostrils as he pressed himself against her. His gap-toothed grin like that of a drunken sailor. His breath was just as bad. He leaned in and whispered into her ear.

"Now, what would make a little lady like you wanna give up yer virtue for a guy like me?" He took off his bowl-shaped cap, his face coming closer to hers. The smell of his breath made her stomach turn.

"Well, a lady certainly does value her life, and I'm quite fond of mine, imperfect as it is." She smiled nervously, her gut twisting with nerves.

"Oh, is that so?" He closed his eyes, puckering his lips to kiss her. She slid down the wall, avoiding his needy, slobbering lips, and fell hard on her bum. She groped blindly once more in search of the Dracosinum, hoping to slip it back into her corset before he noticed.

"Look at you, making promises you can't keep." Lust had blinded him now to everything else.

"Nonsense," she said, "I was just trying to speed things up." She used her free hand to pat the ground next to her, but instead, he grabbed her hands and pulling her to her feet, moved her towards the center of the cell. The Dracosinum remained in the shadows where he would never see it as long as she was able to keep his attention diverted.

"Here." He pointed to the ground, and she sat, trying to fight the tears that threatened to take over. The very thing she had saved when so many others were giving it away freely was about to be taken so she wouldn't be murdered.

"Lay down," he ordered, and she did as she was told. He unbuttoned the front of his trousers before crouching over her. He shoved a knee between her legs, to force them open, and as he did so, she put every hope, every prayer, and every ounce of strength in her knee as she rammed it hard up into his groin.

His eyes went wide with surprise, then he grabbed himself and fell back on the floor with a loud moan. He sucked in a deep breath, trying to yell something at her, but no sound came out. Wylie ran back toward the wall, picked up the Dracosinum, and rushed out of the cell. She took the steps two at a time while the prisoners yelled for her to come back and let them out. When she reached the first landing, she paused and pushed the lever to open the Dracosinum, where Quincy sat silently, a small frown of sadness on his face.

She couldn't even speak, merely nodded at him, and thought herself into the Teselym, her human eyes closing as her human body fell to the cold stone step, the blue flame rising again, and the Teselym body forming around her essence. Not yet at full size, she remained on the landing for the moment, realizing she had not thought out her plan thoroughly. There was no way she would consider leaving her body here unprotected. She would have to take it home, but at the same time, she needed to fight.

"Quincy." His little clockwork body rose from the Dracosinum and fluttered in front of her. "Are you able to take my human body home? It won't be safe here." Quincy never said a word, but Wylie could see a small tear on his face. "I'm okay, please... just get her, er, me, out of here."

He nodded his head, growing in size until he was nearly as big as her, their dragon forms crowding the stairwell and overshadowing her human body at their feet. Quincy lifted up her human form, still remaining silent.

"How...?" she left the question unsaid, for by then he was quickly fading out, and she realized at that moment that there was a great deal more she didn't know about Quincy. If she lived through this ordeal, she would make a point of prying more information from him. She heard the sound of scratching claws and flapping wings, and knew it must be Quincy escaping the horrible jail. She let out a sigh of relief.

It's time to fight. Only this time she would not go out into the open as small as a mouse. She would go out large and she would go out fighting. If the Lieutenant came after her, she would bite him in half; she didn't care about the balance of good and evil. Her dragon's claws made scratching noises on the stairs as she resumed her ascent. As she reached the top, she let out a tremendous roar, scaring the guards half out of their wits. The whole lot of them went screaming out of the police station into the street, and she burst out right behind them.

Immediately Wylie took to the skies, willing herself to control her temper and not light the station on fire, burning it to the ground. When she could no longer see the ground and the moon was her only companion in the sky, she allowed herself to relax. There was something about flying among the soft haze of clouds under the light of the moon that instantly put her heart at rest.

What do I do next? The faint sound of flapping reached her ears, and she whipped around expecting to encounter the Siapheg. Instead, she came face to face with a full-sized Quincy.

"That was impossibly fast," she said, her voice redolent with admiration.

"My darling girl, may I remind you again that I am a piece of the gods themselves?"

"My body?"

"Is resting peacefully in your room at Lord Adrian's, please don't worry. We have much bigger things to deal with currently." As he spoke, he shrank to his normal size until he was no bigger than a butterfly and took his rightful place in the Dracosinum hanging from her neck.

"Now, might I say... dear girl, what you did in there, it was..."

"Stupidity? I should have just let them hang me?"

"No, my dear. I was going to say that it was brave, magnificent, and incredible." His little voice should have felt like music to her ears.

"How was it brave? The police lieutenant knows who I am, he will tell Lord Jameston his version of what happened, and Lord Jameston will continue to come after me until he succeeds in having me killed. He will ruin Lord Adrian, and possibly Lady Judith as well. There will be no future left for them. That is what I have done today!" She opened her mouth wide, letting out a large roar that reverberated through the skies like thunder.

"Quite possibly," Quincy stated simply. "Then again, you are the Teselym, and what you described sounds like evil taking over just a bit too much. Isn't it your job to balance the two?"

She nodded. Not happy with his words, "How am I to fix this, if I cannot kill him? And another thing..."

"Yes?"

"Why didn't you tell me he was the Siapheg? His depth of evil and cruelty show him for what he is. I thought the Siapheg didn't have a Dracosinum?" she spat through fanged teeth.

"I never said that," Quincy replied. "I said that the Siapheg doesn't have one of me. No moral compass, or conscience to speak of. It has only itself and its own desires."

"Yes, and you also said that the Siapheg that exists now is one of the most reasonable you've ever dealt with. Lord Jameston is the one who holds the Dracosinum! I saw him drop it. I held it in my hand. It's just like mine!"

"The Dracosinum is only a measure of time, much like a pocket watch. Consider it a pocket watch for Dragaleths." She could feel him grinning, for when he smiled, she felt it inside. Much like he was a tiny part of her.

"So Lord Jameston is the reasonable Siapheg that you told me of, and he is in possession of nothing more than a

Dracosinum?" she asked again, soaring quietly above the Earth thinking hard about her next move.

"The Siapheg is in possession of the Dracosinum," he stated dryly.

"Very well. If Lord Jameston is in charge of the Dracosinum, then all I need to do to restore balance is kill him so that his daughter can become the next Siapheg." I'll figure out the details once everything plays out. It's time to find Lord Jameston.

CHAPTER EIGHTEEN

As she began her slow descent back to the Earth, Quincy asked, "Wylie, do you know what you're doing?"

"Yes, I do, thank you," her voice was matter-of-fact.

"And are you certain this is the answer?"

"Indeed, I am," she replied. "Thaddeus McCollum's findings stated that the Siapheg and I do not have to kill each other, we are free to live in harmony if we maintain the balance. The balance is off, Quincy. I must kill the Siapheg, who I suspect is

Lord Jameston, and since you won't tell me otherwise, I am going to challenge him. I need to restore the balance."

"Wylie, be very sure this is what you want. Taking a life will hang over your head for the rest of your days. It is a heavy burden to bear whether the victim be friend or foe."

"I am well aware of the decision I make, Quincy. I am also aware that many lives will be ruined if I don't deal with him in this way. I must right this wrong. I must," she argued. Her tone silenced him, and she wondered for a moment if it was indeed the right thing to take on Lord Jameston in Siapheg form.

Of course, it is. This is what embracing your Dragaleth side is all about. Embracing the decisions, you would never be capable of doing otherwise.

Having resolved to proceed with her plan Wylie sniffed the air for his scent, but there was no trace of it. She tuned into her dragon-sense, willing her mind to show her where he was. It directed her to a man who lay bleeding in an alleyway. She grabbed her Dracosinum in her claws and transported to the man's location.

The man was bleeding more heavily than Wylie had originally seen in her vision, his breathing coming hard and raspy. She gently lifted him in her arms, his body already cooling from loss of blood. She shrank to human size and carried him to the nearest locally-run charity clinic. Her Teselym form caused numerous gasps and screams as she entered the place. She placed him on the ground, then she returned outside and took flight.

Another vision came, two men with masks had pistols pointed at a family. She transported to where they were and grabbed the men up by their backsides, dropping them atop a police building, where there was no chance of them getting down, except by firemen's ladders.

"Where are you, Siapheg? Reveal yourself." She yelled out into the night, half-expecting it to answer. She was met with silence.

She wasn't sure what part of the world she was in at the moment and decided that closer to home would offer the best possibility of finding him. He seemed to enjoy striking out at people close to Dobbinsturn. As she arrived over Lower Kinnemore, she heard a man screaming.

She followed the sound until she discovered a fresh trail of blood, which led her to...

The Siapheg!

She landed quietly behind it, her talons not making a sound as she hit the street. She let out a tremendous roar, and the ominous black beast turned to face her, its yellow eyes exuding hatred, and its mouth dripping blood.

For goodness' sake, it has graduated from killing people to eating them? Wylie roared again, and the Siapheg dropped the bit of flesh that was in its mouth and turned to confront her.

"I challenge you to a battle, Siapheg! Your reign of terror stops now," she screamed out, her voice full of rage.

The Siapheg licked its lips, the flash of its eyes reminded her of Lord Jameston. The black monster bared its gleaming teeth before it reared back on its haunches and sprang into the sky.

She immediately gave chase, as fast as she could fly, hoping that the cloud cover would not prevent her from following her foe. "Raaawwwwrrrr…" Something strong and painful bit down on her tail, and the pain shot right up her spine, making her giddy with dizziness. She flapped her wings faster and darted away, spinning in midair to face him head on. He was nowhere to be found, and then she heard something above her.

The Siapheg had flown high above Wylie's head to gain momentum, allowing it to drop like a dragon-shaped arrow, flying directly at its target. In desperation, she flexed her wings trying to propel her body out of its path, but the Siapheg's horned head hit her smack in the middle of her scaled chest.

The two scaly beasts locked together in free fall. With her vision off-kilter, and unable to get her balance back, Wylie felt almost certain she would plunge straight into the ground and be killed on impact.

Using her front talons, she tore desperately at her counterpart's head with all her might trying to dislodge it from her chest. The Siapheg let out a screech as her claws tore a gash on its face. It ripped away from her and disappeared in the cloud cover.

No, no, no! she thought.

"Show yourself, coward." Pain nailed her square in the back, and she was sent flying, spinning like an empty wine barrel rolling downhill. She was getting dangerously close to the ground. She whipped her tail wildly in an effort to slow her rate of descent. At the last moment, before she hit the street, she was able to spread her wings wide. Using the cobblestones as a jumping off point she propelled herself skyward once more. The Siapheg was directly in her path, and as he turned to attack her, she dodged her head to one side and clamped her teeth down on his neck.

The rusty taste of blood instantly filled her mouth, nearly gagging her. She shook her head like a bull terrier, tearing a huge chunk from its throat. The Siapheg stopped fluttering its wings, and its tar black body plummeted Earthward. Wylie spat the flesh from her mouth, detesting the taste of blood. She preferred not to watch the Siapheg splatter on the cobblestone, even if it was Lord Jameston. She waited until she heard the sound of the impact before she set her wings and soared quietly to the Earth.

Search as she might Wylie found no sign of the Siapheg's body. The dust cloud that had arisen from the impact slowly cleared, enabling her to make out the rough outline of where her counterpart had hit the ground with a terrible force. As the dust and debris settled, a tiny blue flame appeared. It paused momentarily as if waiting for her. Then suddenly it took off in a straight trajectory over the homes and alleyways of Dobbinsturn Parish.

As the blue flame approached Lord Jameston's estate, Teselym Wylie, smiled in satisfaction, I was right! Her thoughts were cut short as she watched the flame move toward a second story window on the right side of the Victorian manor. That window led to Judith's bedroom. No… no… no… it isn't possible!

The flame went right through the closed window, so Wylie, shrinking herself in size, grabbed her Dracosinum and transported herself into the room of her friend. In silent dread Wylie pattered over to Judith's form on the bed, gently pulling her over onto her back. Judith's chestnut hair was in wild disarray, partially concealing her face. The blue flame now descended on Judith, causing her chest to rise and fall with one final breath.

Wylie rested her scaly, taloned hand on Judith's arm, and stood there until her body grew cold. The realization that she had been the one to harm her friend so violently made the human part of Wylie sick to her stomach.

Judith? Judith was the Siapheg. Wylie saw that the Dracosinum still hung around Judith's neck. She hooked the chain of it with her claw and gently tugged it off over her head. Quincy had been right about killing weighing heavily on her, she should never have taken on the Siapheg. Her blind human hatred for Lord Jameston had cost her dearly.

Forgive me, Judith. I've made a terrible, terrible mistake.

CHAPTER NINETEEN

Stumbling backward, not believing what she was seeing, Wylie hadn't realized the sun had begun to rise. Quincy emerged from the Dracosinum and fluttered noisily next to her, his tiny watch gears whirring.

"Miss Wylie, the sun rises, and you are mere moments away from the end of 'The Time of Dragons.' I suggest you get home, and now!"

Wylie couldn't move. She was paralyzed. Her best friend lay murdered in her bed, and Wylie was the one responsible. How can I live with myself? How can I continue to be the Teselym when I have committed such an evil act?

"Wylie!" But it was too late. Wylie's Teselym body was fading with the rising of the sun. Soon there was just the flickering blue flame of her essence hovering near Judith's bed. "Don't worry, Wylie, I'll take you home."

Then Quincy grew larger in size and opened her Dracosinum. He spoke some unintelligible words, some magic incantation she assumed, as she found herself being propelled toward the device until she was safely inside.

"Wait!" She tried to say but having no body or voice box she had to be content with thinking the words. Wait, I need Judith's Dracosinum. Quincy picked up on her thoughts immediately as he always did and though she couldn't see him, she felt herself being lifted and the sound of a chain being shifted. Good, he's grabbing her Dracosinum. The next moment, they were in her room at Lord Adrian's estate.

Quincy opened the Dracosinum, allowing Wylie's essence to escape and re-enter her human form. Once she was human again, she sat on the edge of the bed and cried. The fight with the Siapheg played itself over and over in her mind. She had murdered Judith.

MURDERED.

MURDERED.

MURDERED.

Wylie, supposedly the balance for good, had murdered her best friend. She felt she would die before she could be forced to bear the burden of that for all of eternity. She sobbed great wracking sobs that let out all the pain she had somehow managed to keep bottled up since her father's death, compounded by her near ravishment by the guard, and now the murder of her friend.

When she ran out of tears, she had a pounding headache, and all she wanted to do was sleep and never wake up again.

She grabbed up the Dracosinum and threw it on the floor. The dragon wing cover popped open, and Quincy, who had been sitting silently next to her while she cried, finally spoke.

"Are you alright, Miss Wylie?" he spoke softly, barely audible to the human ear.

"You lied to me! You lied to me!"

"Never, my dear, I am not capable of such a thing."

"You told me that the Siapheg was in possession of the Dracosinum!" She screamed at him, throwing her pillows across the room.

"And that was indeed true. I also asked you if killing the Siapheg was something you wanted to do, and you assured me it was. You said you couldn't restore balance until the Siapheg was dead because you assumed it was Lord Jameston..."

"Yes! Why didn't you tell me the truth? Why didn't you stop me? Why didn't you tell me that Judith was the Siapheg? I would do anything to have her back. Surely, I am now eviler than she. Aren't you supposed to balance good and evil? How is letting me take her life going to accomplish that?"

Quincy tsk tsk'd, as he paced back and forth on her bed.

"Before you blame yourself or me, Let us examine the facts more carefully. First of all, you are not meant to be perfect. If you were perfect, the balance of good would far outweigh the bad. You are still human. Secondly… might I point out how many deaths have occurred because of her?"

"Four?" Wylie responded.

"That you know of, Wylie. Now that she is gone, I can tell you that she has killed no less than thirty-three human beings to feed her appetite. That person you saw her feasting on tonight was the thirty-third one."

"I thought you said this Siapheg was one of the more level-headed ones you have dealt with? How can that be!?"

"You know that I cannot tell you the details, Wylie. I can assure you that I have reasoned with her a time or two. I can tell you that she seemed adamant about only taking the lives of those guilty of atrocious acts."

"You couldn't tell me that?" Wylie yelled angrily.

"I said she seemed adamant before about that, but I can tell you as of late, her stance has changed. It started with the killing of your father and the captain you heard about. Those occurred on the same night. It was all downhill after that." He paused for a moment while Wylie thought over what he was saying.

"So you're telling me she was a bit of a vigilante? She was trying to balance good and evil on her own?"

"In her own way, Wylie. But that was never her battle to fight, and it destroyed her. To place the weight of good and evil on one being and expect them to balance the two, without a moral compass to guide… is too much of a burden to bear. She paid for that with her life, so regardless of whether or not you can see that, it needed to be done. Imagine how many more lives she would have taken? The gods have already foreseen it, and it is not appealing."

Wylie was struck silent for the moment, so Quincy continued.

"She cared a great deal for your father and knew that he wasn't as capable as he used to do because he was sick. She tried though, in her own way, she tried."

"She knew my father, I mean... she knew it was him?"

"Yes, Nicolas didn't know that she knew, but Judith followed us home one night. No rules against that... she watched as we entered your home. I heard her thoughts, knew it was Judith and knew how close she was. She thought it was you at first until your father started lagging. The illness he had, made him weak in dragon form as well. Once she pieced two and two together, she tried to help."

"By killing people?" Wylie said incredulously.

"You see the problem?" Quincy's eyes had grown downcast.

"Why didn't you tell me?"

"My job is to tell you what is right and wrong when you can't seem to balance the two. If I had told you that the Siapheg was your best friend, would you have killed her?"

Wylie didn't even have to think about; she knew that she would never have hurt Judith intentionally.

"I wanted to kill Lord Jameston." Wylie broke into tears again.

"Get dressed, Miss." Wylie didn't have the energy to argue, so she grabbed her clothes. "If you had killed Lord Jameston, it would have been for all the wrong reasons, and that would have further upset the balance of evil more than he and his daughter had already done. By killing her, you not only set the balance back and stopped her vicious and unnecessary killings, you have also struck Lord Jameston right where it hurts. Now, if I were you, I would go take advantage of the situation, before that man destroys the only home you have ever known, permanently."

"But I don't understand! Why was Judith the Siapheg? Her father is still alive. Why was he carrying the Dracosinum?" She turned her head to face Quincy.

"First, have you not seen how controlling her father is? Do you sincerely think things would be any different with her being a Dragaleth?" Wylie shook her head 'no.' "Next, let me quote for you that handy little book you obtained from Dr. Mullings. By the way, I knew the man who wrote the journal that Thaddeus found, but that's neither here nor there."

"A Dragaleth must remain a Dragaleth for a minimum of ten human years before passing the bond onto another sibling or child unless killed beforehand. The gods determine who carries on the bond if there is more than one eligible family member. When an old Dragaleth dies, regardless of the cause, the bond immediately passes on to the next of kin. The Dragaleths do not have to kill each other; the ideal is that they dwell in harmony, and they must only maintain the balance of good and evil. If at any point, the balance dips farther towards good, or further towards evil, the opposite Dragaleth may challenge his or her counterpart to a battle in Dragon form."

"There, you see?" Quincy asked.

"So, you are saying that Lord Jameston was the Siapheg for ten years, and then he passed it on to his daughter?" Quincy nodded his head.

"The moment she was done nursing the cad."

"You can't be serious?"

"Oh, but I am. I meant it when I said she was the most level-headed Siapheg I have ever dealt with. Reasonable, intelligent, from the moment she first flew. Granted, she needed a lot of help back then, the only time I was allowed to step in. But she is the exception to the rule. It's just sad that as a child she didn't know what was happening to her. She used to wake up and tell her father about her nightmares. You know, he placed that the Dracosinum in her room every night at the same time, and took it back every morning at the same time? At least, until she was of age."

Quincy continued, "It's a horrible thing, helping a child do evil. Something I won't soon forget, and you can best believe that the gods have quite the special punishment for Lord Jameston. Anyway, now you must return his Dracosinum to him. Since there are no other family members, the Dragaleth duties revert back to Lord Jameston. He won't be happy about it, but you may use your new position of power to make sure that he never steps out of line again. It may bode very well for you."

"Now you're allowed to tell me things?"

"This is different. It's been an unbalanced night, and this is the last step in the program, sort of the last cog in the gear you might say. Besides, I am not crossing any lines or I wouldn't be able to say anything. Now hurry. He will be headed here shortly. He's just received word of his daughter's death and has murder on his mind. Better deal with that before it gets out of hand," he cautioned her.

"Yes, yes! Right away." She wiped the tears from her face, and grabbing both Dracosinums, she transported herself to Lord Jameston's house.

Standing outside on the step, she heard slamming of doors and shouting from inside. She knocked heavily on the door.

"What!" Lord Jameston had flung the heavy teakwood door open, and when he saw her face, he pulled out a large double-barreled pistol and aimed it at her. "You! You did this!" He cocked the trigger back and aimed it at her chest.

"Before you shoot me, I have some information about who murdered your daughter." The admission stopped him in his tracks.

"What do you mean?"

"I mean, Lord Jameston, I saw it happen as I was there." She pulled the Dracosinum that belonged to him out of the pocket of her father's frock coat.

"This is yours, I believe? A family heirloom?" He froze.

"Where did you get that?" he hissed.

"How about you put down your gun, and I mean way down? Put it somewhere you can't use it right away. Offer me some tea, and you and I will have a nice friendly talk. Unless, of course, you'd rather I hang onto this for you?"

He scowled and shook his head.

"Hildreth, be a dear and get our houseguest some tea. Oh and take care of this while you're at it."

Hildreth came bustling in from the kitchen, a look of surprise on her face when she saw Wylie. She looked from Lord Jameston to Wylie several times before she took the pistol from his hand and hurried to the kitchen to make tea.

"We'll take it in the parlor," he called after her, then led Wylie through to a luxuriously decorated room. The parlor screamed elegance and class, and she found herself surprised but delighted.

"Come, let us sit, and you can tell me what you know."

The chairs were high backed and covered in red velvet. After the stress of the past few days, it felt heavenly to sit on something so softly padded.

"Lord Jameston, I know what you are. I have come to offer you a peace treaty."

He shook his head. "You're going to have to explain yourself better than that. You are headed for the gallows in a few short hours. How did you escape?"

"Oh, I'll get to that part. Just let me finish," she said.

"Well, you'd better hurry. I have a murderer to find and your death to look forward to."

Wylie pulled out her Dracosinum and placed it and Lord Jameston's side by side.

"Here is the truth, Lord Jameston. I thought that the Siapheg was you, and I wanted you dead. So I challenged the

Siapheg to a battle last night. I killed the Dragaleth by tearing out its throat. So giddy was I that I had defeated you that I was devastated when I found out it was Lady Judith instead. She was my best friend, more like a sister really. So now, you have not only taken my home from me, and nearly my virtue, but also my best friend, and almost my life. So, I have one thing to say to you."

She stood up and stared him directly in his eyes.

"Since you are the Siapheg once more, I order you to give back the homes to my people. Call off the police from myself and Adrian, and then you will leave town. If you do not keep the peace and do as I say, I will find you and I will kill you. It is your job, oh aging Lord Jameston, to do evil but not here.

"I understand, that is who you are… but your time in this town is over. If you so much as breathe on this part of London again, you will not live to see another day. I loved your daughter like family. But you, I have no concern for. I will make your death slow and painful. You have until tomorrow." She nodded her head at him and stormed out of the house, slamming the front door so hard it rattled the windows.

When she was out of sight of the house, she took out her Dracosinum and transported to Lord Adrian's. The front door was open, and a police wagon was parked outside. Worried that Lord

Jameston had already started to come after Adrian, she ran inside the house.

"Adrian, Adrian!" she screamed.

"Wylie?" He jumped up from the settee and ran to her. "You're out of jail? How did you manage that! We heard you'd been sentenced to be hanged." His face, which moments before had been pale, now flushed with color. "I thought I had lost you too, I just can't take any more loss," he said as he pulled her to him.

In the room they had enjoyed a meal in the day before, many men and women were standing around somber-faced.

"Judith has been murdered." Lord Adrian spoke softly. "I am so sorry, Wylie."

"I know Adrian. I have just come from Lord Jameston's house."

"You what? Is he the one who freed you?" Adrian asked.

"Not in the slightest, just give me a minute."

Lord Jameston appeared at the door just then, his normally kempt appearance somewhat awry, his shirt tail hanging out, shirt collar undone, and his frock coat flapping open sloppily.

He smelled strongly of alcohol, but as he stumbled into the house, he looked Wylie straight in the eye.

"I'm out of here. Lugwallow now belongs to the people." He tossed some papers on the floor. "There's everything you need. I was on my way to speak to the lieutenant, but I just got word that he was murdered last night as well. So I am off to settle some debts at the station. Then I'm leaving town." He stumbled out of the door, and everyone rushed to see him climb into his personal carriage, his driver taking off before he had even got seated properly.

Wylie rushed over to grab the papers from the floor.

"This declaration states that Miss Turpin owns the property located at..." Wylie thumbed through each paper, every family had their name on their property, and the Vicar himself had signed it.

"How did he manage this so quickly?" Wylie stared at Adrian in disbelief. She had only just left his home, not less than an hour before.

"I imagine that a man with the kind of money Jameston has can do almost anything he wants, in any time frame that he wants." Wylie remembered the quick transportation that came with the Dracosinum and realized that Lord Jameston had embraced his duties again, and was using the Dracosinum to fulfill her demands as quickly as possible.

Good. It's time that monster of a man did something positive for once.

CHAPTER TWENTY

Wylie soon found out that rumor on the street was that Lord Jameston knew who killed his daughter and the police lieutenant and that he'd left town to go after the guilty party. Of course, Wylie knew better. She had not laid a finger or a talon on the police lieutenant, but it was no small victory that her best friend Judith's last horrific act had been to kill and eat parts of the very lieutenant who had tried to take Wylie's virtue from her.

Fate had no doubt stepped in. Among other kindnesses, Lord Adrian graciously paid to have Wylie's father's body relocated to his family cemetery where his own father's remains were interred. He also ordered several bouquets of roses and placed them in honor of Lady Judith and Nicholas Petford, the two people that Wylie had loved so dearly. He made sure they were both given funerals fit for royalty. Lord Adrian had truly surprised her in many ways.

It would take them some time to fully recover, but the people of Lugwallow were so overjoyed to be back in their homes, that it hardly mattered that Lord Jameston's men had ransacked them.

Shortly after moving back into their homes, Lord Adrian arranged to help them clean up their small parish.

Through his generosity, the people of Lugwallow Parish were able to restore Lugwallow to its former glory. Wylie's love for Lord Adrian grew, though she thought it imprudent to act on it too soon after the death of her friend.

Wylie continued to work for Lord Adrian for the time being. She did, however, refuse his offer to live in his house, or even in the servant's quarters. "I have a home of my own," Wylie protested. Adrian continued to plead with her to make the move, pointing out that she would be far more comfortable than her own home and she wouldn't have so far to walk to work. She made many excuses, but her primary concern was preventing Lord

Adrian from finding out what she really was. "No, I've lost a lot of things, but I still have my pride," she argued.

"How can I let you live this way? Surely, you can't expect me to be okay with this." He indicated her surroundings. Wylie feigned insult and sent him on his way that evening.

He apologized later and never brought it up again though he didn't promise not to keep trying.

On another day, in another conversation, Adrian said, "Wylie, I love you, and I want nothing more than to have you near me and under my protection."

"Adrian, you know that I love you, but the people of Lugwallow still need me. When the time is right, we will be together."

Wylie had read nothing in the journal or the notes that Thaddeus McCollum had left behind, that spoke of love, or marriage, or families. She didn't feel right about all of this yet, not that Lord Adrian had actually asked for her hand in marriage. As winter approached, and men came in and out of town helping to make the necessary repairs, Wylie awoke one morning to a gentle tapping on her door.

"Lord Adrian." She smiled from ear to ear, when she answered the newly installed mahogany door, the soft smell of the wood teasing her nostrils. Wylie was grateful that his visits had become more frequent since the whole ordeal, and the door was an expensive gift to prove his affections.

"Do you remember the first time I came here?" he handed her a bouquet of lilacs before stepping inside.

"I certainly do. Totally inappropriate. Not that I'm completely innocent of that day." She laughed softly, remembering the look on the widow Turpin's face when the woman had questioned her about her gentleman caller.

"Oh come now, Wylie. You can't tell me that you didn't know we would end up together."

"Well, we aren't quite together yet, are we?" she teased.

"Yes, a fact that has haunted me day and night from the moment you left my home to return here." His face grew somber. "I want you to come home with me. I want you to live in my manor as a lady of the house of McCollum."

"Oh, is that so?" She raised one eyebrow as she walked to the small table he had provided her and laid her flowers on it. Then she turned to face him, hands on hips.

"Yes, that is so," Lord Adrian grabbed one hand from her waist, held it in his, and knelt in front of her. His top hat slid forward as he searched his pockets for something. She took his hat off with her free hand, to prevent it from falling to the floor and placed it on her head.

Her action made Adrian laugh, and struggling to compose himself, he held out a small black velvet box.

"I had this made for you, in hopes that you would honor me by becoming Lady Wylie McCollum." He took the ring out, and set the box on the floor, took her hand and slipped the ring on her petite but calloused finger. "It's perfect."

"Adrian, if I say yes… there will be consequences. You have to know that." He took the hat from her head and placed it back on his own.

"Would those consequences include stealing my hat?" he joked with her.

"No, I just… I have so much to tell you."

Adrian stood up, and grabbed her right hand in his, "Does this have anything to do with…. with… the dragon thing?"

Wylie gasped.

"How do you know?" The color drained from her face.

"Don't worry, I haven't said a word to anyone. I suppose I always knew there was something different about you. Chaos doesn't respond so favorably to many people."

"What do you mean by that?"

"I mean, that dratted horse is even temperamental around me, and I've had him since he was a wobbling little foal. Around you though? He's always been a bit of a puppy dog." Adrian laughed. "You think he lets me nestle him the way you do, arms around him, and all?"

Wylie smiled wide, "No, I suppose I haven't ever seen the two of you interact that way. I've never really thought much about it. I thought he just understood me."

"Oh, I have no doubt he does to an extent. I think it's more than that though."

"So that's how you knew?" she questioned.

"No, not that. It just always struck me as odd. I'll be brutally honest with you, even though you may not like what I'm about to say."

"I'm sure there is nothing you can say that will be equal to the things I have done or what I need to tell you." Her gaze was intense, and she wondered how long he would stay around once she confessed to him.

"Well, the next clue that something was a little off…" Little beads of perspiration were forming on his forehead, his face reddening.

Is he… embarrassed?

"I assure you this is not how it sounds."

"Out with it, Adrian," she urged.

"A few months ago, the night Judith died, when your neighbors took up temporary residence at my estate, I found myself having yet another sleepless night. I was worried about you and was trying desperately to figure a way to get you out of jail. Typically, at times like that, I get up and go work on the carriage, but that had already been completed, and I had nothing else to take my mind off things.

"Wanting desperately to see you, or at least assure myself that you were safe, I went to your room. I knocked as if you were inside, and the door swung open under my touch. Your bed was empty as I'd expected, though it broke my heart. I had hoped that the horrible events of the day were all a dream.

"Realizing that I was possibly never going to see you again, alive, I sat on the edge of the bed. A lot of thoughts ran through my mind that night, Wylie… and they weren't good thoughts. If you hadn't run Lord Jameston out of town, I'm not sure I wouldn't have done something to him myself." Storm clouds invaded his eyes, just then, and she wanted desperately to kiss them away.

"He's gone, my love, he's never going to bother us again."

"Yes, I know, but I can't help wondering whose life he is ruining now?" Wylie shrugged and brushed a stray hair from his forehead.

"Anyway, the whole situation was too much. Losing you, the thought of you being hung to die at daybreak, it tore me apart. I sobbed like I've never sobbed before, the thought of a life… without you?" he leaned forward and kissed her forehead.

"Let's just say that I had a lot of dark thoughts that night. Then, in the middle of that… as I sat in the darkened room, with not even moonlight to highlight the shadows… I heard the window lock jiggle. Worried that someone was breaking into the room, I rushed downstairs to grab my pistol and hurried back as quickly as I could.

"When I entered the room the second time, someone was lying on the bed. I pointed the gun at the stranger, wondering how they got into my house, then I heard a noise at the window again. The curtains were open then, moonlight streaming in, so I rushed to close it, my mind still not processing anything that was happening. As I closed the window, I saw something I would not have believed had I not seen it with my own eyes.

"A dragon, a little green dragon, was flitting away, and as it flew away, it grew in size until it nearly blocked out the moon. It disappeared into the clouds, and I just stood there like a dolt, staring after it until I realized there was a stranger sleeping in my house. Forgetting to close the curtains, I hurried back to the bed and shook the stranger who was fast asleep.

"Wake up! I demanded, but the stranger didn't budge. I grabbed an arm and flipped the person over, and it was your beautiful face I found myself staring at. So help me, I wanted to lift you up and kiss you. I wanted to beg you to tell me how you'd escaped and ask if you'd seen the dragon? Was it all a dream?

"I wanted to ask you how you got back, not realizing it was the dragon who had brought you. I did something completely imprudent at that moment, and so far out of character for me."

"What, Adrian? Tell me..." her heart had begun to speed up, and the slightest hint of fear nibbled at the back of her mind... surely he hadn't?

"The moonlight was streaming in through the window, and it cast the most delicate glow across your face. You looked so beautiful, I just had to..." Adrian hung his head in shame. "I had no control of myself, it was like I was in a trance. I sat next to you on the bed. Your tangled hair framed your face so perfectly, you looked angelic. You didn't stir, and all I could think about was how beautiful you would look in a wedding gown. I wanted to whisk you away then and there, and carry you to the nearest church and demand the vicar marry us, hell be damned for what Lord Jameston would do to me.

"I knew you would have a story to tell when you awoke, and I wanted to make preparations in case Lord Jameston came after you in the morning, as I am sure he planned on doing as soon as he found out you'd escaped. So I kissed your face and left the room, shutting the door behind me. As I hurried about the house looking for anything that would help me get the comeuppance on Lord Jameston, the vision of the dragon hit me again.

"I had seen a real, live dragon, the stuff of fairy tales. The stuff of imagination. Had I lost my senses? Then I thought about how your return coincided with the dragon, and my imagination got the better of me. I came up with all kinds of theories. Maybe the dragon was an angel, and the gods knew how much I loved you, and they returned you to me? Maybe your father died and became a dragon, and that was him rescuing you?" he laughed.

"Oh, that's just scratching the surface. There were so many ideas. So many ludicrous and childhood fairy tales, but I dared not say a word to anyone. So I bottled it up. It was not the right time or place to ask you or anyone about mythical dragons flying around at night. As far as I knew, my grief had caused me to hallucinate, and you had climbed in the window of your own accord, and that was the truth I accepted for the longest time."

"So what changed your mind?"

"Beside the fact that the first time I saw you after that, you were changed into new clothes and entering my home through the front door? Do you remember when I held you and told you that Lady Judith was dead?"

"Yes, I remember."

"You'll never know how totally confused I was at that moment. I had seen you asleep in your bed. After staying up all night thinking about the dragon and how to defeat Lord Jameston, only to have an officer at my door early in the morning, and the next time I see you, you are fully clothed and coming in from Lord Jameston's house? How was that even possible? I never saw you leave.

"That set the gears in my mind turning, even though I felt like I was going completely mad. So after we buried Judith and your father in my family cemetery, I knew there was something off. For a time, I tried to shrug it off... tried to pretend that things were normal. When you rejected my offer to stay in my servant's quarters, even though you wouldn't be a servant, it was just a way to have you close to me until it was right for us to marry, I knew it had to do with this... whatever this is.

"Then, as I visited you here in Lugwallow, and you acted so mysteriously each evening as the sun went down, I assumed you either didn't love me or that you had something to hide. Please forgive me, Wylie, for what I am about to say, but I had to know. I had to find out for sure. For goodness sake, I was beginning to wonder if you had another suitor."

Wylie gasped. "Why would you say such a thing?" She withdrew her hand from his and stepped back. "Even when I was just your stable hand, you were always more than an employer to me." Her heart pounded furiously against her ribcage. It felt like a stab in the gut that he had not trusted her completely.

"Wylie, my love, please hear me out. I have experienced all there is to experience in the past few months. Please... I didn't know what to think. I was ready to commit myself to an asylum."

The tone of his voice was desperate, like that of a man lost at sea, begging to be rescued. She nodded her head at him, urging him to go on, as she fought to hold back tears.

"I did something I'm not proud of, in a moment of complete desperation. I rode Chaos home after one of our evenings together, and then I walked back here and sat just a few feet away in the alleyway just beyond the widow Turpin's home and I waited. I waited for another carriage to pull up, a man to come knocking on your door… I don't know what I really expected or what I would have done had that happened.

"Instead, as I sat on the dirt-covered ground, the chill seeping into my bones, and the grime staining my trousers, I saw something that I can only describe as magic. The most beautiful creature that I have ever beheld, aside from you, emerged from your house and just like the dragon that had brought your body back to the room at my manor, this beautiful white dragon grew in size as it took to the skies.

"I watched dumbstruck, overwhelmed, and completely at my wit's end. Either what I saw was real and I, Lord Adrian, now realized that there is indeed magic in the world. Or I was losing my mind and I needed to walk, no run, to the nearest asylum. I sat there all night, freezing, unable to move for fear that I would wake up and discover that I was indeed crazy.

"Then, as the softest light of morning began to tinge the sky, the magnificent beast returned, and as it got smaller, I saw it grab something from around its neck and disappear, just near your house. Now, I'm not as intelligent as my father was, but it didn't take much for me to link the disappearing and reappearing to the device. It was a few more days before I finally accepted that the dragon had something to do with you, as well as the green dragon I had seen before that I assumed had rescued you from jail.

"I imagine that device has something to do with you leaving my home the day Judith died, and returning again so suddenly. Am I correct? Now, what pieces am I missing exactly? Can you fill in the blanks for this simpleton?" Adrian laughed gently, and though she had been hurt that he had not trusted her, she immediately forgave him.

"It gets worse, I'm afraid." It was Wylie's turn to drop her head and feel ashamed.

"My love, it's not that bad. It will take some getting used to... and I'm still trying to wrap my mind around it, but it's nothing to be afraid of. So you're half dragon? People in love have married with much worse problems." He stepped toward her, placing fingers beneath her chin, and raising her face up so he could look into her eyes.

"I'm afraid it's much worse, my dearest Adrian. Do you also know that I am the one who killed Judith?" Those words caused all the color to drain from Adrian's face.

"No! Tell me it isn't true."

"I'm afraid it is. Wait there a moment, please."

Wylie ran off to her room to get the journal and opened it to the illustrations which now had her own notes attached to them.

"Here… maybe this will help you understand." She thrust it at him, then retreated to the kitchen table to sit and wait. He followed her and sat at the table across from her while he opened it and began reading.

After a while, he stopped and looked up at her, "McCollum. That's my last name."

"I know, I originally thought you were the Siapheg."

"Would you have killed me?" he asked.

"No, how could I? Read the part about how they can challenge one another to a battle. Death is only necessary if the balance is skewed too badly, and one side or the other has gotten completely out of hand. I then thought Lord Jameston was the Siapheg and he had thrown everything out of balance."

"So, why did you kill Judith?"

Wylie began to sob, the memories of her best friend's death as fresh as if they had happened yesterday, even though it had been several months by this time.

"You have to believe me, Adrian. I didn't know… I truly didn't know. I thought it was Lord Jameston. Don't you see? I was trying to restore the balance," she confessed. "There's so much more to it, Adrian. She killed people. So many people. She…"

Wylie lost control, and then Adrian got up and sat next to her, putting an arm around her.

"Hey, it's okay." He squeezed her tighter.

"I know it's a lot. You can walk out now if you want…" Wylie managed to whisper to him.

"Wylie, you know it's not as easy as that. I love you. Even if you were the Siapheg, I would love you. This doesn't change anything for me."

"Really?" she said, brightening up.

"Yes."

"Then what do we do?" Wylie asked, her tears subsiding as she realized that sharing the truth about what she was hadn't sent him running for the hills.

"It's a lot to process, but I can hardly imagine what it's been like for you, dealing with all of this on your own. I mean… if what I read is true, and I would never think you a liar, it must be a heavy burden to bear."

"Oh Adrian, you have no idea. Judith... my best friend… I mean…" She couldn't even find the words to express her sorrow.

"Wylie. You don't need to worry about it. We're going to figure the rest of this out. Together." The statement was simple, matter-of-fact, but the weight it lifted from her shoulders was immeasurable. She was almost afraid to ask her next question.

"Do you still want to marry me?"

"Absolutely! Why wouldn't I?" He picked her up and swung her around. "But what's your answer?" he teased.

"Yes! I'll marry you!" she wrapped her arms around his neck.

"Excellent! Because I am headed to the United States of America by ship to show off my steam-powered carriage. A wealthy gentleman there got word of my design and wants to buy it from me, for more money than I have ever seen. Will you come with me?"

"Sure! It might be fun," she said.

"Yes, it might be," he said with a grin. Then he kissed her and swung her around again. "Can you imagine, seeing the States for the first time?"

She didn't have the heart to tell him that she transported there almost every night recently. Obviously, there were a lot of things he didn't understand yet. She would have to rectify that situation once they were married.

One step at a time.

GLOSSARY

Black Maria: A slang term for a police van used to transport prisoners, originally these were horse drawn and so could take some time to arrive at a crime scene.

Carbon blaster: Pistol

Chavy: Child

Chiv, shiv: Knife, razor or sharpened stick

Dobbinsturn: Well-to-do part of London, fictional.

Dracosinum: A magical device used to measure the hours one may remain a Dragaleth. Also houses Quincy, while not in use.

Dragaleth: A race of dragons created specifically by the gods to retain an equal balance of good and evil in the world.

Essence: The spiritual being of a person, their soul, who they are.

Flush: prosperous, rich.

Full as a tick: very drunk.

Gallies: Boots

Gas-pipes: A term for especially tight pants.

Grenadier guard: Is an infantry regiment of the British Army.

Haggersnash: A person who is full of spite

Lugwallow: Very poor part of London, fictional

Mafficking-An excellent word that means getting rowdy in the streets.

Mutton-shunter: A policeman.

Quincy: A magical dragon made of clockwork, sent from the gods to act as a conscience for the Teselym. A magical being capable of changing size and camouflaging (this includes invisibility, changing colors, and more.)

Refulgent: Shining brightly; radiant; gleaming:

Rip, Reprobate: "He's a mean ol' rip." noun

1.   A depraved, unprincipled, or wicked person: adjective

2.   Morally depraved; unprincipled; bad.

Siapheg: Black dragon of the race of Dragaleths, made manifest in human bloodlines.

SIAPHEG

Teselym: White dragon of the race of Dragaleths, made manifest in human bloodlines.

TESELYM

Usciere: Venetian cargo vessel.

BIBLIOGRAPHY

Bird, Christopher. The Grandiloquent Dictionary. 10th ed. N.p.: Chris Bird, 2010. Print.

McCarthy, Erin. "56 Delightful Victorian Slang Terms You Should Be Using." Mental Floss. Erin McCarthy, 6 Nov. 2013. Web. 01 Jan. 2017.

Metrov, D. A. "Victorian-Steampunk Glossary." Metrov Fine Art Paintings and Prints Santa Barbara Contemporary Art Contemporary Paintings GODDESS Movie Project Environmental Films Victorian Steampunk Glossary Comments. Metrov, n.d. Web. 01 Jan. 2017.

History.com Staff, History.com Staff. "Crusades." History.com. A&E Television Networks, 2010. Web. 23 Jan. 2017.

History.com Staff, History.com Staff. "Black Death." History.com. A&E Television Networks, 2010. Web. 23 Jan. 2017.

Woodford, Chris. (2007) Steam Engines. Retrieved from http://www.explainthatstuff.com/steamengines.html. [Accessed (February 8, 2017)]

"reprobate". Dictionary.com Unabridged. Random House, Inc. 20 Apr. 2017. <Dictionary.com http://www.dictionary.com/browse/reprobate>.

McAlpine, Fraser. "Five Horrible Diseases You Might Have Caught in Victorian England."BBC America. N.p., 2013. Web. 15 Feb. 2017.

Newman, Simon. "Doctors in the Middle Ages." Doctors in the Middle Ages | Middle Ages. The Finer Times, 2008-2017. Web. 04 Apr. 2017.

Wikipedia contributors. "Black Maria." Wikipedia, The Free Encyclopedia. Wikipedia, The Free Encyclopedia, 12 Oct. 2016. Web. 20 Apr. 2017.

Wikipedia Contributors. "Grenadier Guards." Wikipedia, Wikipedia, The Free Encyclopedia, 28 Mar. 2017, https://en.wikipedia.org/w/index.php?title=Grenadier_Guards&oldid=772653614. Accessed 20 Apr. 2017.

Wikipedia Contributors. "Horse Transports in the Middle Ages." Wikipedia. Wikimedia Foundation, 17 Nov. 2016. Web. 02 Apr. 2017.

If you enjoyed what you read, feel free to follow me on

FB: https://www.facebook.com/authorasanderson/

Twitter: https://twitter.com/AuthorASAndersn

Instagram: https://www.instagram.com/authoraanderson/

Personal Website:

http://authorangeliqueanderson.com/

Blog:

https://authorangeliqueanderson.wordpress.com/

Author central on Amazon

https://www.amazon.com/Angelique-S.-Anderson/e/B00WHCDCEU

And if you really enjoyed it, please make sure to leave a review! Thank you so much!

Enjoy this free preview to Eden's Demise

Chapter One

Break Out

Mr. Lars Morello, one-time big shot corporate bigwig and former CEO of Plant Harmonics, had sunk as far as he could go, and he knew it.

Sitting alone in his jail cell, the smell of mold pervaded his senses. He scanned the flat gray surface of his lackluster surroundings for the hundredth time. The sensation of doom that came from being in a place like this overwhelmed him, and he hadn't even been here a week. Every day, it felt as if the gray cement walls were closing in.

He wasn't throwing in the towel, not just yet. No iron bars were going to stop him from doing what he needed to do. As the saying goes, he was down but not out.

The metal cot beneath his thinly clothed backside felt like a bed of nails. Thoughts of revenge roared through his mind like a ferocious lion. Two names kept running through his head, like hamsters running on a wheel. Adam and Evelyn would be the first to pay. But they wouldn't be the only ones. No one was going to toss him into a cell like a piece of garbage and live to tell the tale.

Adam may have taken his company from him and thrown it to the dogs, but he would rule an empire once more. All the hours spent in his cell, plotting his revenge would be hours well spent if everything went according to plan. He sat upright on the side of his cot, hands gripping the frame as he waited impatiently for his morning meal.

Lars tapped his barefoot on the cool concrete. I am still the greatest inventor of all time. I created immortality!

"Maybe I let all that power go to my head, but I know damn well I don't deserve to be in here." The darkness was his best friend lately. Always listening, always waiting, with its cold empathetic embrace. "I don't deserve to be here. I don't deserve to be wasting away in this cell. May as well give me the electric chair…" he continued out loud. There was no one to acknowledge him. Not even the scurrying of rodents to break the silence. He cursed out loud, irritated with his predicament.

'Ting,' 'ting,' 'ting,' came a gentle metallic tapping on the door of his cell. His 'home sweet home' didn't come with a porch light, so the early A.M hours were as black as sin. He linked his fingers together prying backward and applying pressure until they popped.

"Lars… you in there?" came a hushed voice. Seriously?. Of course, I'm in here, where else would I be?

"No, I decided to take a midnight stroll."

"Don't be a smart-ass. I've got what you asked for." If his blood could have stopped flowing, or his heart could have stopped beating, even momentarily, it would have at that very second. Is it possible? He thought to himself. If he weren't afraid of waking the other prisoners, and giving himself away, he would have jumped from the squeaking bed frame, and run to the bars, yelling triumphantly. Instead, he got up slowly and steadily, his feet protesting as he crossed the cold concrete.

"You've really got it?" Lars whispered, his mind enraptured at the thought that his time behind bars, had not been in vain.

"Yes, here." A hand reached through the small gap between the bars. He could barely make it out in the pitch blackness, but as he reached for it… his fingers clasped a cool thin vial. He snatched it from her, forcing himself not to yell out in excitement. Bringing the vial up to his ear, he shook it and could hear the gentle sound of liquid sloshing inside.

Eden's Serum.

"And what about the plans?" Lars ventured.

"That depends… What are your arrangements as far as monetary compensation?" the woman hissed back.

"What we agreed on… five."

"Hmm…. I just don't know if five is going to cover it."

"What do you mean, you don't know if it's going to cover it? That's what we agreed on. You're the one who set the price if you recall."

"No, I'm sorry, I don't remember. I think ten would be more reasonable."

"Ten?" Lars answered back incredulously. "What the hell do you mean, ten? That's total B.S, Vosburg, and you know it."

"Eh, suit yourself. Now you have your Serum and nowhere to go. What are you going to do with it in a prison cell? Doesn't do anything for you, unless you can get out of here, right?" the woman retorted.

"Fine. Fine. Ten million. You better damn well get me out of here, and to somewhere safe, or I'm not giving you a penny." From the shadows beyond the bars, the tall sandy-haired woman smiled with cobra-like venom.

"Hey, I aim to please handsome. I'll have you out of here before the end of the day, but you better mind your manners and talk nice to me, or I'm going to have to charge you extra."

In the dark, Lars's eyes went wide.

"That's pretty low."

"Says the man who killed hundreds of people for monetary gain. Now shut up before you wake everyone up. I have things to do, things that involve getting you out of here, remember?"

He plodded back to his bed to lie down, twisting the vial in his fingers as he awaited his release.

What's a few million for my freedom? Once I carry out my plans, I'll be THE richest man in the world.

Chapter Two

Fake Out

Katelyn Vosburg stood outside the warden's office, and knocked softly.

"Who is it?" his voice boomed out.

"Vosburg."

"Enter."

She turned the knob, entered the room, and closed the door behind her, locking it.

"Anyone out there?" he asked

"Officer Charleston, but he's busy dealing with something."

"Where is everyone else?"

"At their desks."

"Very good." Warden Halloway got up from behind his desk, came around the front of it and sat down on the edge, crossing his ankles one over the other. She hated that he looked so good in his uniform. "What did you find out?" he asked.

"He agreed to the extra cash."

"Oh yeah?" He stood up, and walked over to her, towering above her by just a few inches. "That's a good girl," he said, grabbing the sides of her face, and sticking his tongue in her mouth.

Pig. She thought, as she kissed him back. His time is coming too.

Another day had passed behind the concrete walls, and Lars was no freer.

"Dammit," he muttered the word over and over, as he sat waiting on his bed. He had even drifted off to sleep a few times.

Where the hell is she?

The words seemed to act like a summoning spell, as seconds later he heard footsteps coming down the hall.

Keys jingled outside the door of his cell, and Vosburg walked in.

"I need you to stand up and put your hands behind your head Lars. You're being relocated." Obediently, he stood to his feet, and placed his hands on his scalp.

"What the Hell is going on, Vosburg, I thought you agreed to get me out of here yesterday?" he growled.

"What are you, stupid? I told you what was happening, now do what you're told, or we may have to accidentally 'misplace' you on the way. Got it?"

He wanted to blow the lid off the place, and if he ever got out, he was going to do just that. He had now added officer Vosburg to his list of people who needed to die first.

"Hag," he muttered under his breath.

"Oh no, honey. I'm your worst nightmare. I can't wait to get your scum sucking ass out of my prison," her voice carried a note of superiority.

"What's with the attitude, Vosburg?"

"Do you ever shut up?" Lars closed his mouth then, secretly thinking about all the ways he could kill her.

She locked the handcuffs on his wrists too tight, which pissed him off even more. He almost went off on her, then thought better of it. It was clear by her behavior that she was in an extremely foul mood, and she was also the one with the gun. He wasn't about to set her off more than was necessary.

She pushed him out into the hallway, where two other officers were waiting. Each grabbing an elbow, they began carting him off. Almost as an afterthought, she walked to his bed, and reached under his pillow. Sure enough, he had left the serum there.

"What an idiot," she mumbled, then marched out of the cell, shutting it quietly behind her so as not to wake the other inmates. She caught up to the officers who were detaining him. Together they headed towards the warden's office, where a uniformed guard was waiting.

"Have you filed the correct paperwork, Vosburg?"

"Of course, Charleston."

"Just making sure. I don't want the warden coming down on you." She grimaced at his response. Just hearing the word 'warden' ticked her off. Every fiber of her being wanted to see that man get what was coming to him.

"Yeah, I appreciate it. Thanks."

He smiled, and tipped his hat to her.

"No problem, ma'am."

If only the warden was a little more like Charleston, she would have felt differently when he'd first come on to her. Now, she constantly felt like an insect trapped in a web she couldn't escape. She was forever waiting for him to descend on her, and suck the life out of her as he monitored her every move.

She tapped on the door to the warden's office.

"Vosburg?"

"Yes sir, I have Deacon and Peterson with me."

"And the prisoner?"

"Yes Sir," She raised her voice to be heard through the door. Despising the fact that she had to call him sir. He demanded respect, which by her estimation, he didn't deserve. He insisted on having his every whim catered to, but she was quickly reaching her limit. For the time being, she would do what she needed to keep him happy, knowing that the cogs had been set in motion to bring him down. He would never force himself on anyone else. Not after she was done with him.

The door opened suddenly, and he came out.

"Very good, let's go down to transport. I have a vehicle and an officer waiting."

She nodded solemnly and followed him, the two officers holding the prisoner followed suit. Once they reached the transport area, Lars was forced into the rear passenger compartment of an armored vehicle. The automatic lock clicked into place as the door closed behind him.

"Officer Davenport, I am going to need you to stay here. The only person I trust with prisoner Morello is officer Vosburg."

"But I need to get back to my facility," he argued.

"I'm aware of that. I will make other arrangements for you, or you can wait until she gets back." Warden Holloway answered.

"What? No, I need to return the truck."

"Don't you trust my officer?"

"No, it's not that. There's a set protocol to follow… you… you're breaking protocol!"

"Listen you little bastard, when you're here, you work for me. Got it? I said I don't trust anyone else with this prisoner. So as far as I'm concerned, that is the only protocol I need to follow. You want to whine to your superiors about it, go ahead cry baby. I have things to do, and you're cramping my style. Now either shut up, and get your wimpy little butt inside, or walk back."

"Davenport, why don't you head inside with us? We can figure something out," Officer Deacon suggested.

"Very well, but I'm doing so under protest." Davenport jumped out of the vehicle, and stormed into the building like a child throwing a temper tantrum. Vosburg took his place behind the wheel of the truck.

"Now, hold on a second, come back down here," Vosburg cringed inwardly. Damn Halloway. She should have known it wasn't going to be that easy. Sliding down from the truck, she stayed behind the door, so that even though it was wide open, she could pull it in on her, if necessary. He approached her, and just as she started to pull the door, he stopped it.

"Are you trying to hide from me?" He took a look over his shoulder to make sure the other officers had gone inside. There was no one around. "You're not upset with me, are you baby? Didn't I do what you wanted?" He stepped in close and pressed his body against hers, kissing her neck. "Damn girl, you smell good." It took everything in her, not grab the back of his head and yank his face into her knee. His hand made its way to her shoulder, and slid down her front.

In a split second, she drove her knee up into his groin as hard as she could. She made solid contact, and he stumbled backward yelling in pain.

"Shit!" he said as he collapsed to the ground. She hopped in the truck, and slammed the door. She saw him mouthing a few choice words as she backed out, but she didn't care. Warden

Holloway was going down and letting Lars escape would be only the beginning of it.

Lar's neck hurt from being jostled around so much, and he was fuming mad from having been deceived. What the hell was Vosburg trying to pull, anyway? It must have been a good hour or two before he finally felt the vehicle slowing down. The vehicle hit a couple of large bumps that sent him airborne, bouncing around in the back of the truck like a ping-pong ball. Then stopped, suddenly. He heard a crunching sound right before his body hit the floor.

"Ow! Dammit!"

He felt battered and bruised. All he could do was lie on the cold metal floor of the back of the truck, where he'd landed and groan. He could hear the front door of the vehicle open and slam, then the door to his compartment opened. Full glaring daylight poured in, and it took his eyes a minute to adjust.

"Come on jerk off, we don't have much time."

"Where the hell are we?"

"Middle of nowhere, sorry about that." She stepped up into the cab and helped him to his feet. "I had to make it look like something ran us off the road." She left his handcuffs on him, as she led him away from the truck.

They were in a rough wooded area, and as he looked back, he could see the tire marks through the shrubs and bushes. His eyes followed the tracks to the vehicle which had plowed into a tree. The front was crushed in, but not too badly.

"How did you manage to not hit anything else on the way in here?"

"Pure dumb luck, I guess. Look, we don't have much time. I'm going to need you to run as fast as you can with me. I know for a fact that truck has an electronic tracker on it, and they may be no more than a few minutes behind us. We need to get out of here. I have a safe place for us to go, but it's going to take some real effort to get there.

"Are you going to take my handcuffs off?"

"Not yet, you're just going to have to trust me. If we get caught out here, it's in our best interest if it still looks like you're my prisoner."

Lars let out a string of obscenities.

"I know, life sucks a big one. Now let's get the hell out of here." She grabbed his arm, and they took off running in an easterly direction away from the accident. Her heart had never beat so fast in her whole life. She wasn't sure what the warden was capable of, but if he had managed to get the okay for a female to work at an all-male prison, and had managed to get a transfer for the most hated man in America, then no doubt, he was capable of some pretty evil voodoo.

Chapter Three

Underground

Lars and Officer Vosburg ran on and on for hours, stopping for short rests from time to time. Lars was not happy about the less than regal treatment. He had expected by now to be returned to his status as it was before his beloved Plant Harmonics shut down. As nightfall approached, and his hunger started to get the better of him, he stopped running and sat on the ground.

"What are you doing?" Vosburg demanded.

"I'm starving."

"So am I! We're almost there."

"I want to eat," he insisted, folding his arms angrily across his chest.

"You're acting like a child. Get your ass up and let's go."

"Not until we eat." Vosburg undid her gun clip, and pulled it out of its holster. She pointed its business end at Lars.

"Now get up off the ground and get moving. We're almost there, but you're going to have to trust me."

He grumbled as he struggled to get to his feet, impatient with his clumsiness. She grabbed the crook of his elbow and hoisted him up.

"We can walk for a bit, it shouldn't be more than another mile or so."

He cursed at her under his breath.

"Better watch yourself, Lars. Until you pay me, I'm in charge. When your debt is settled, you can do whatever the hell you want. Also, I have just upped my fee."

"Bet you're...."

"Ah... ah... ahh...... watch your mouth around a lady. Or so help me, I'll leave you here and radio for help. Warden Holloway will disregard anything you say, if he believes it will get him into my pants. I'll bet you anything I could have him lock you up and throw away the key."

"Oh, I know he likes you," he hissed, his gaze falling to her breasts. She smacked him across the face, leaving a glowing red mark.

"Don't even." She pushed him ahead of her, and stuck her gun in his back. "Since you want to be a smart ass, instead of this nice little companionship we could have had, you get to be in front.

Make any wrong moves, and my little friend here gets to scramble your insides. Savvy?"

He didn't say a word, but nodded his head, and stomped onward, anger emanating from every pore. He couldn't wait to pay her off so he could have his life back.

It took them about a half hour more trudging through the woods, struggling through brambles and stumbling over deadfalls, before Vosburg stopped. She holstered her gun, and walked a few steps ahead squinting at the ground. Kneeling, she pushed away some leaves and vines, and finally found what she was looking for. Lars could see a silver handle beneath the shrubbery. Is that a door in the ground? He found himself experiencing an extreme case of Déjà vu.

"What the Hell?"

"Told you, you could trust me." Vosburg brushed aside a thin layer of vines and other detritus, uncovering a small metal panel. As she did so, a familiar looking, scanning device rose up out of the ground.

"Identidisk machine! I assumed those were all destroyed?"

"Oh, they were. The technology to create them was not. There were only a small handful of these ever made, primarily in preparation for your return. I think you will be quite pleased." She pulled out a delicate silver chain that hung around her neck. A small tree with green emeralds swung from the bottom of it, and she waved it over the identification system. "There have been some changes, since you last saw the design. We've made it a little less obvious, the chips are smaller, and they contain less personal information. As you can see, it looks more like tasteful jewelry now."

After reading her chip, the machine descended back into the ground with a metallic click, followed by the sound of pneumatic compression, as a submarine style hatch rose out of the ground. As it did so, all of the vines and undergrowth shifted like pieces of a puzzle unlocking themselves.

"I really would like to take your handcuffs off now, as the passage down is a bit narrow. Problem is I don't trust you, yet. What are you going to do to change that?"

"What's down there?"

"Why Lars, it's your very own lab. To do with as you will, but we assume that you have great plans for Eden's Serum. Am I correct?"

"We?"

Vosburg let out a hearty laugh.

"Just wait and see!"

If you enjoyed that sample, be sure to check out:

Eden's Serum: Book One in the Eden Series

Eden's Demise: Book Two in the Eden Series

Little Lost Girl: The Complete Series

And other work released by Angelique S. Anderson

Thank you for your support!

74786983R00177

Made in the USA
Columbia, SC
06 August 2017